THE GLADE MANOR
MURDER

Also by Elizabeth Lemarchand

Who Goes Home?
Light Through Glass
The Affacombe Affair
Alibi For A Corpse
Death of an Old Girl
The Wheel Turns
Troubled Waters
Cyanide With Compliments
Change for the Worse
Death on Doomsday
Nothing to do With the Case
Step in the Dark
Suddenly While Gardening
Unhappy Returns

THE GLADE MANOR MURDER

Elizabeth Lemarchand

Walker and Company
New York

Published in the United States of America in 1989
by Walker Publishing Company, Inc.

Library of Congress Cataloging-in-Publication Data

Lemarchand, Elizabeth.
The Glade Manor Murder / Elizabeth Lemarchand.
p. cm.
ISBN 0-8027-5741-3
I. Title.
PR6062.E5G541   1989
823'.914—dc20   89-32449
CIP

Printed in the United States of America

10 8 6 4 2 1 3 5 7 9

To F.K.M.

THE GLADE MANOR
MURDER

List of Major Characters

John MORLEY   *Live at Glade Manor,*
Buckford, near Brading,
Rose MORLEY, his second   *Downshire*
wife

Emily GOVER ('Nanky')   *Nanny and then housekeeper*
at Glade Manor

Adrian MORLEY   *John's older, adopted son, an*
Oxford don

Richard MORLEY   *John's younger son*
Gail MORLEY   *Richard's wife*   *Live at Dower House*

Jeremy CRABBE
Amanda CRABBE, his wife   *Friends of the MORLEY*
Henrietta LEGGE, of   *family*
Loxford

Stephen ASH   *New owner of Hob's Cottage*

Walter RIPLEY   *A solicitor in Brinkleigh,*
Northshire

Mr SWAN   *Manager, Northern Counties*
Bank

Chief Superintendent Tom POLLARD of Scotland Yard
Chief Superintendent LOOSEMORE of Brading
Inspector Gregory TOYE of Scotland Yard
Inspector BOSWORTH of Brading police
Detective Constable HARPER, Scotland Yard driver
P C Ted WILLIS of Brading police
Chief Constable of Downshire
Assistant Commissioner
Matron of Nightingale Nursing Home
Joe DADDS   A tractor driver
Harry BANKS   Van driver for Little's Paints

Chapter 1

Walter Ripley, senior partner of Swan, Ripley & Cornhill, solicitors of Brinkleigh in Northshire, began to
collect up the passport and papers on his desk and gave
his client a brisk professional smile.

'So, Mr Ash,' he concluded, 'now that we've got your
identity confirmed we can get on with the business of the
money and personal effects your great-aunt Mrs Clara
Firth left you.'

He broke off to ask over the intercom for Mrs Firth's
suitcase to be brought in.

Stephen Ash sat facing him across the desk, lounging
back in his chair with legs crossed. He was a thickset man
in his early 60's, sun-tanned with dark hair dusted with
grey and beginning to recede a little. In contrast to Walter
Ripley's impeccable dark suit he sported well-worn
casuals over a crumpled white sweater.

'Where did you get the gen?' he asked, a slight nasal
twang in his voice.

'Oh, from a number of sources,' Walter Ripley replied,
searching in a drawer. 'Your birth certificate to start with.
School and war records.' He extracted a labelled key,
glanced at it and put it down on his blotter. 'The Australian
immigration authorities. People you worked for when you
first went out ... Thanks, Paul. Put it down here, will you?'

The young man who had brought in a small old-fashioned green portmanteau deposited it by the desk and withdrew. As the door closed behind him, Mr Ripley shot a keen glance at Stephen Ash. He held out a silver box of cigarettes.

'You don't? Sensible man. Nor do I. Well now, to recap briefly, this firm drew up a Will for Mrs Firth in 1947. As you know, she lived over at Cranforth, and her Bank there, the Northern Counties, dealt with any investment or tax matters for her. Mr Swan, the bank manager, remembers that she struck him as a cagey type, anxious that her affairs should not leak out at Cranforth. That perhaps is why she asked us, and not the local solicitor, Mr Hargreaves, to draw up her will. It was very simple, leaving you, her great nephew, everything she died possessed of, and appointing this firm as her executors. The Will was lodged with us. Nothing was heard from her until 1970 when she wrote to say that she had sold her house and was going into a Cranforth nursing home. We had her file out and wrote to ask for your address which she had given in her Will as the same as her own.'

Stephen Ash's eyebrows rose sardonically.

'Well,' Walter Ripley pursued, 'we wrote at once for your present address and got no answer, nor one to a follow-up letter. So in the end I went over to see her and find out if she was in touch with you. I found her perfectly *compos mentis* — remarkably spry for 89 — but couldn't budge her an inch. She said you had never bothered to send her a line since you left England, and she had given instructions in a letter which the matron of the nursing home had been told to let this firm have at her death. In it she stated that enquiries as to your whereabouts were to be put once, and once only, in the leading Australian papers. If there was no response everything she left was to go to the Salvation Army.'

Stephen Ash guffawed. 'Well, anyway, I've beaten the Salvation Army to it. I must say it's staggering that she gave me the chance of scooping the pool. She was my father's aunt and married a bloke who manufactured buttons and whatever, and made a pile. They had no kids, and he died sometime in the early 1930s leaving her the lot. She'd always disapproved of my parents' marriage and we hardly ever saw her. Dad had a go at touching her for my school fees but only got a dusty answer. Both my parents were killed in a car smash just before the war. I let her know about the funeral and she came along, but cleared off afterwards without speaking to me. I was just eighteen, and with no other known relatives, so the obvious thing was to join up for the duration.'

Walter Ripley, nearing retirement, regarded his client with interest through thick-rimmed spectacles.

'Did you tell Mrs Firth that you had enlisted?'

'Nope. No bloody business of hers. Surprisingly I went through the whole show without a scratch, and knew that the one thing I wanted was to get clear of the mess-up of post-war Europe. Australia seemed to fit the bill, so I collected my gratuity and the bit Dad had left me and a few personal papers and pushed off. Somehow family quarrels seemed a bit petty after the sort of things I'd seen, so I wrote her a few lines and gave her the address of a bank in Sydney. No answer. I thought she might be dead. Anyway, she just faded out of my mind as time went on.'

'How did you make out when you got to Australia?' the solicitor asked.

'If life had gone on without the war I'd have trained as an architect. I'd always fancied something in that line,' Stephen Ash replied. 'Too late to start training by the time I got out there, though. I got myself a job with a

3

building firm and worked my way up as time went on. I own a small bit of property by now. Saleable stuff, even if there isn't all that much of it.'

'Are you going back?'

'Not now, seeing I've come in for a bit from Aunt Firth. About £30,000 clear you said, didn't you?'

'About that.'

'I fancy buying an old cottage in a cheap property area, and doing it up myself. Cut out labour costs that way.'

'Of course, Mr Ash, if we can be of any help to you over the purchase of such a property?' Mr Ripley suggested, his professional instincts aroused.

'Thanks a lot, but it's too bloody cold up north here after Sydney and it's only November. I'm going for something further south.'

'Quite. The West Country or somewhere on the coast, well away from the affluent south-east, perhaps?'

'Yeah.' Stephen Ash jerked back his head. 'God, talk about a chance in a thousand! That I saw your advert, I mean. I don't spend much time on the papers, but just happened to pick up one in the departure lounge of Melbourne airport while I was waiting for my flight back to Sydney to be called, and my eye chanced to hit my own name. It was like getting the hell of an electric shock ...'

'Incredible luck,' Walter Ripley agreed. 'Now, about the money. We decided to allow a period of three months to elapse. Old newspapers do turn up. Wrapped round fish and chips, for instance. Meanwhile we lodged the cash after Mrs Firth's estate was wound up in the local branch of the Northern Counties Bank. The manager's a very decent chap and glad to give you any assistance you want. Shall I give him a ring and see if he could see you this morning?'

'Sure. I want to get a move on. I'll have to go back to

Sydney briefly to settle my affairs before house-hunting here.'

'There's just one other matter before you go,' Walter Ripley said a few minutes later as he replaced the receiver. 'Miss Firth sold most of her possessions before going into the nursing home but kept a few personal belongings. Books and photographs, for instance, and a packet of letters and papers. They're in this case for you to have a look at in case there's anything of family interest that you'd like to keep.'

He hoisted the portmanteau on to his desk, unlocked it and threw back the lid.

Stephen Ash looked unenthusiastically at the neatly packed contents.

'OK,' he said. 'I'd better take it back to my pub and have a look through the stuff, I suppose. I'll drop it in on my way to the bank, and come back here this afternoon to settle up with you people. Thanks a lot for all you've done for me, Mr Ripley, and I mean that.'

The business at the bank took longer than he had expected. He recognised know-how when he encountered it, and took the manager's advice on the most profitable temporary disposal of his legacy until his plans for the future were more settled. When this was agreed there was barely time to get to Swan, Ripley & Cornhill, and settle his account with them before the office closed. He debated foregoing the payment he had made in advance for dinner, bed and breakfast, and catching the last train to London, but decided against the idea. Even if you had just come into thirty thou' there was no point in chucking cash away for no sensible reason.

Alyswin Hotel where he had booked in for a night was small, uninspired and redolent of past meals. He had a quick drink at the bar, collected his key and went up to his room. He dumped Clara Firth's portmanteau on the bed, pulled up one of the two hard-backed chairs provided and began operations by tipping out its entire contents in a confused heap.

Actually, he decided, there were a few possibilities among the junk. A silver-backed dressing table set, for instance, and a small carriage clock. Oddments of clothing such as embroidered nightdresses went into the wastepaper basket: the chambermaid could be told to help herself to any pickings she fancied. A bible and prayer book went the same way, but an unexpected little cache of old-fashioned jewellery including a diamond ring was carefully transferred to his own suitcase. It was not until he had almost arrived at the bottom of the portmanteau that he came on a packet of letters tied up with faded pink ribbon. He stared at the pale old-fashioned handwriting of the topmost envelope. Old love letters? Or just one old girl blathering to another? Perhaps he had better just glance through them . . .

There was nothing of the remotest interest in the first half-dozen. It was not until he had deciphered the first couple of pages of the next letter that he came upon a piece of news quite casually conveyed that immobilised him . . .

He was still staring at the faded handwriting on the creased and folded sheet of writing paper when there was a knock on the door. A young waitress enquired with a nervous giggle if the gentleman was taking dinner.

Chapter 2

Glade Manor, home of the Morley family since the early nineteenth century, stood on a wooded hillside overlooking the valley of the little river Weaving about three miles west of the village of Buckford. Lower down the slope a branch of the drive led off on the right to the small attractive Dower House of mid-Victorian date. Since the death of John Morley's elderly widowed mother some years previously it had been occupied by his son and daughter-in-law, Richard and Gail Morley.

The Weaving was the southern boundary of the Glade Manor estate. On its far side with a gate on to the Buckford road was Hob's Cottage, vacant since the death of its owner some months previously. With its small neglected garden it already had a derelict appearance. Stepping stones in the Weaving, submerged after a rainy spell, suggested a former link between Manor and cottage.

Gail Morley, perusing *The Times* on an evening early in March by her sitting-room fire, caught the distant but unmistakable sound of her husband's car. Gyp, a black-and-white cocker spaniel asleep on the hearthrug, raised his head, giving a small excited whimper and beginning to scramble to his feet. Tyres scrunched on gravel. A car door slammed and seconds later came the sound of a latch key in the lock of the front door.

'Oy!' Gail called.

Richard Morley appeared at the door, a tall fair young man in his late twenties.

'Stow it, old boy,' he adjured the leaping yelping cocker. 'I'm back.'

He stopped to kiss his wife, and pulled another chair up to the fire.

'What kept you so late?' Gail asked, manoeuvring a drinks trolley closer.

'Hugh Mandeville brought that 1576 *Decameron* down himself. He's an interesting bloke. About the mid-fifties, I'd say. Money written all over him in block capitals, but surprisingly well-read and knows quite a bit about books. Their material make-up especially.'

Since the beginning of the century the Morleys had built up a select and successful enterprise for the restoration of valuable books. The small works occupied premises in Buckford, and the firm's clientele included eminent bibliophiles and institutions. John Morley, now in his 60s, was progressively passing more of the management on to his son Richard.

Richard picked up a bottle and looked enquiringly at Gail.

'Dry martini, please darling,' she said. 'Do go on. What sort of job is it going to be?'

'Hefty and time consuming. Basically it's a superb edition but in a ghastly state. Mandeville found it under a lot of junk in a cupboard under the stairs at Gatherton Castle.'

'How come, for heaven's sake?'

'Old Lord Mandeville died last autumn at 97, apparently having refused to have anything at Gatherton touched for about twenty years. His only son — our chap's father — was killed in the Normandy landings, and his widow seems to have been *persona non grata* with

8

the old boy. Our chap seems to have been more or less ignored by his grandfather and devoted his energies to money-making in the City. He married money, too, apparently, and the idea is to clean up Gatherton and live in it. There's a little Mandeville at Eton.'

'A good thing that there's plenty of lolly,' Gail said, holding out her glass to be refilled. 'It sounds as though the *Decameron* restoration job's going to be pretty expensive.'

'Mandeville remarked that we must have something on account and wrote out a cheque for a thousand, unasked.'

'Lumme,' Gail commented.

'You'd better come over and have a look at the thing tomorrow before we start on the job. If you can get away in Nanky's absence. You got her on to the train at Brading this afternoon, I take it?'

'Yes. The funeral's on Thursday morning which leaves her tomorrow for sorting and packing her half-sister's belongings. Not that there can be many since the poor old dear's been living in an almshouse for years. Then Nanky catches an afternoon train back on Thursday, getting in at 6.20.'

'The obvious thing is for me to meet her. I'll go straight from the Works.'

'OK. The daily women up at the Manor are putting in a bit of extra time while Nanky's away, so Rose can cope all right.'

Nanky, officially Miss Emily Gover, was an integral part of the Glade Manor set-up. John Morley was still unmarried at the time of his demobilisation in 1945, and returned immediately to deal with the arrears of business that had accumulated since his elderly partner's death a year earlier. It was during a visit to London that he chanced to meet Fenella. An orphan from an early age, she had been brought up by a spinster aunt recently deceased, and on demobilisation had taken a temporary job at Harridges while attempting to plan her future. John Morley, going into the store on impulse to make a purchase, almost unbelievably found himself falling in love with her at first sight. Her response had been hesitant, but she eventually accepted him and they were married by special licence in London. His reappearance at Glade Manor with a bride was the sensation of the year in the neighbourhood. Fenella's shy charm and responsiveness to the welcome she received resulted in her rapid acceptance by John Morley's circle, and she was quickly received into its life.

Time slipped by, and only one thing marred the happiness at Glade Manor: Fenella remained childless. Finally, after five years of unproductive medical advice, she and John decided to take the step of adopting a baby boy, and in due course a suitable candidate was found. His parents, members of the professional class, had been killed in a car crash. The Morleys named him Adrian, and after careful investigation Emily Gover was installed as his nanny.

With the not uncommon irony of fate 18 months later Fenella became pregnant, and in due course Richard joined Adrian in the nursery. When the time came for him to follow the latter to a preparatory school, Nanky stayed on at the insistence of John and Fenella as part of the Morley household. A small flatlet was made for her, and she organised the activities of daily women from the village and fulfilled her lifelong ambition of becoming a first-rate cook. It was not until Adrian was in his last year at Oxford that the tranquil regime of Glade Manor was abruptly shattered. Fenella had a sudden fatal heart attack.

During the trauma of the period that followed Nanky

was a tower of strength to the family and particularly to John Morley. Three years later she discreetly added her persuasion to that of Adrian and Richard over his marriage to Rose Ingram, herself a widow, who had been Fenella's closest friend. The success of this step was due in no small measure to Nanky's tact.

Time passed. Adrian did brilliantly at Oxford and embarked on an academic career. Richard joined his father in the family firm in the nearby village of Buckford which handled the restoration of antique and valuable books. He married Gail Lethbridge, who had been one of his contemporaries at Cambridge where both had read history.

Richard and Gail sat on by the fire over their drinks in contented relaxation, casually discussing other topics.

'Must you go up to Town on Friday?' he asked presently.

'Yes, I think so. The searches I ought to be doing are piling up, I want to be as free as possible when Adrian's down over Easter.'

She and Richard had met at Cambridge where both were reading history. Gail had developed a keen interest in genealogy, and subsequently done some useful research in this field. She was Secretary of the Southshire Historical Society which had a surprising number of overseas members, particularly in the USA. The latter were enthusiastic about tracing British forbears and Gail had frequent requests to carry out searches into family history at St Catherine's House Kingsway.

After a time Richard stretched and yawned.

'Let's go and eat,' he said. 'I'm ravenous. With Mandeville coming I only had time to nip out to the pub for a couple of sandwiches and a beer.'

'All laid on,' Gail said, getting to her feet. 'Lamb chops and gooseberry pie. The last of last year's.'

'Lead me to it,' Richard replied, following her to the door round which Gyp was peering anxiously.

Morley's Book Restoration occupied a converted warehouse up a side turning off the main street of Buckford. Gail arrived in her Metro on the following afternoon and walked into a small active world of intermittent varied noises and a familiar composite smell of paper and allied substances, leather, solvents and glue. She was a familiar figure at MBR, as the works were habitually known, and stopped for a few words with some of the employees who were old friends. Going on to the upper floor she arrived at John and Richard Morley's working quarters and the firm's offices.

John Morley looked up and smiled as she came in. War service in North Africa and the loss of his first wife had left their mark on him, but in build, features and colouring there was a strong resemblance between Richard and himself, and also to several of the portraits of earlier generations of Morleys that hung on the walls of Glade Manor.

'Come along in, my dear,' he said. 'Good of you to give Rose back-up in Nanky's absence. You're going to enjoy lending a hand over this job we've just landed. We've spent the morning prospecting and are discussing the dismembering of the corpse.'

Gail sat down beside Richard on the chair he had pulled out for her and contemplated the book lying on the table. It was smaller and bulkier than she had expected, with an outer cover of badly stained and grubby parchment of some sort.

'Impossible to tell at this stage if we can restore anything of the original cover,' John said. 'Some sort of red leather from the look of it.'

'Fortunately the spine's in fairly good condition,'

Richard commented, picking up the book and handing it to Gail who examined it with interest. 'We'll have to take the whole thing to pieces, section by section.'

She opened it and exclaimed with surprise at the Papal *imprimatur*.

'This isn't the original edition. Not surprisingly *emendato* as a result of the Council of Trent,' John explained. 'It's amusing that one or two of the little drawings which embellish the opening capital letters of the chapters seem to have been given a miss. See here.'

They all laughed. Gail asked if many pages were missing and learnt that it was impossible to know definitely until the sections had been separated and checked.

'Job for you if any are,' Richard said. 'I can see you scouring the copies at the BM and Bodley and similar establishments for us.'

'Fun,' she replied. 'The sort of job I like. I only hope there are a few gaps.'

The conversation moved on to chemical analysis of the many stains on the *Decameron's* pages and the most suitable methods of repairing tears in the rather thick paper.

'I must go,' Gail said at last. 'I really must check over the searches I've undertaken to put in hand for earnest American members of the Historical Society. I want to deal with them at St Catherine's House tomorrow. By the way, Richard, we're having supper at the Manor tonight. Rose insists, and her Mrs Cluett's putting in an extra evening.'

It proved to be a particularly enjoyable evening, made all the more so by a telephone call from Adrian at Oxford where he held a Readership in Classical Archaeology at Athanasius College. Rose had written to bring him up to date on family news. His questions about the Mandeville commission landed by MBR and Nanky's temporary

13

absence were interspersed with light-hearted banter with Richard and Gail. Later, as she walked home with her husband under a frosty sky brilliant with stars she felt an upsurge of affection for the Morley family. It was abruptly replaced by a hope which as yet she had hardly dared to admit to herself. Before their marriage she and Richard had agreed to allow themselves a couple of years to settle down and concentrate on MBR and her own writing before starting a family. It was three years ago now that they had decided to embark on their first child. In due course hope had given place to anxiety. The family doctor had referred them to a specialist. No medical explanation had been found for Gail's failure to conceive a child. They were assured that it was early days ... counselled to persevere ...

Now, for the first time she was experiencing a sense of hope. Too faint to be confided to Richard as yet ...

On the following morning she went up to London on an early train, as planned. Settling herself comfortably in the corner of a first-class compartment she opened her briefcase and extracted her notes for a final run-through.

The only other occupant of the compartment was a middle-aged man in the corner opposite to her own. He studied her with interest from behind his copy of *The Times*. Not a conventional good-looker, he thought, but a face quite easy on the eye ... good brow ... firm, but not aggressive chin ... good hairdresser and country clothes of a decidedly pricey brand ... wedding ring ... combining matrimony with some rather high-level career from the look of it.

Suddenly conscious of his scrutiny Gail glanced up and he was abruptly absorbed in his newspaper, but not before registering a pair of fine hazel eyes under well-shaped eyebrows. Accustomed to appraising scrutiny from rather older men she reverted to her notes, disinclined to spend an enjoyable railway journey in conversation with a type almost certainly on a different wavelength from her own. Finally she returned her notes to her briefcase and extracted the *Guardian*. After a time her attention wandered to the landscape flowing past the window. It had a curious rotating appearance, she thought, dark hedges swinging past in rapid succession like the radii of rotating circles, the lightly frosted fields between them forming segments. At irregular intervals a huddle of buildings broke the sequence with a brief shattering roar. Her thoughts reverted to the hope which was beginning to form a constantly recurring background to her mind.

Presently she glanced at her watch. They were making good time. As the encroachment of suburbia became more and more apparent an inevitable conversation about the reliability of the train service and the probable taxi situation at the terminus was launched from the opposite corner. It was a relief to learn that her travelling companion was making for the City, and the risk of laboured conversation in the taxi queue evaporated. After the exchange of a few conventional remarks as the train slowed down he proffered her formal assistance in descending to the platform at Waterloo, politely raised his hat and was engulfed in the stream of arrivals making for the barrier. Gail's spirits rose as she joined it. They were in on time. With any luck she would get through her programme at St Catherine's House without any hold-ups and catch a reasonably early train back to Brading. Back to Richard and the warm family circle while still secretly nursing her hopes. Back to the enjoyable work ahead on the *Decameron* now being dismantled at MBR.

In a surprisingly short time she reached the head of the taxi queue and a few seconds later was en route for St Catherine's House. On her arrival there she found a surprising number of people having their enquiries dealt with. As an established genealogist, however, she was quickly recognised and in a short time was discussing the searches that she wanted made with a senior official. On hearing that she had only come up for the day he promised to get at least some of the information for her by the afternoon. She then went on to look up a number of references in connection with her own work, and went out for a belated lunch. On returning in the early afternoon she found a larger collection of potential researchers demanding attention than ever, and was obliged to join the tail of the queue for the member of staff who had helped her earlier in the day. It moved forward slowly. She had reached the second place when she was abruptly startled into attention by the official dealing with the man at the head of the neighbouring queue.

'Mr Stephen Ash, isn't it? Here's the copy of the marriage certificate you applied for from the Registrar General ... Mr Stephen Ash to Miss Fenella Plume, on 14 July 1944. Right? Good. The fee's five pounds.'

Gail froze into immobility. The man addressed as Stephen Ash was of medium height, sun-tanned, and in late middle age. He was wearing a substantial tweed overcoat. She watched him accept the certificate and hand over a five pound note with a few comments in a slightly nasal accent. At this point her own queue moved and she found herself at its head. Controlling herself with all her will power as the man pushed past her on his way out, she conversed with the helpful official, paid for the certificates that had been completed for her, and managed to extricate herself.

She turned thankfully away and made for a vacant chair, realising that she was — probably absurdly — quite shaken. She made a business of stowing away the certificates in her briefcase as thoughts raced through her mind. Fenella was not all that uncommon a Christian name for a girl, but she had never come across 'Plume' as a surname before meeting the Morleys and getting to know Richard and the family. The London telephone directory would show if there were a reasonable number of examples. Glancing at her watch she saw that it was just on half-past three, a perfectly reasonable hour to pack it in and make for home. Seclusion in a taxi suddenly appeared intensely desirable. Hurrying downstairs and out on to the pavement she managed to flag one down in under a minute.

'Waterloo, please,' she said rather breathlessly as the driver leant over to open the door for her. She thankfully sank back on to the seat and closed her eyes. The preliminary stages of the rush hour were already under way. The alternating spurts of speed and jolts of abrupt braking seemed to shake her back into normality. Arriving at Waterloo she paid off her driver with a generous tip and hurried into the vast echoing vault of the station, heading for a row of telephone kiosks. Maddeningly they were all occupied, but within seconds a man erupted from one of them, leaving the door to swing to behind him. She hurried inside, shutting it behind her and seizing the L-R volume of the London directory. Her hands were a little unsteady but with some fumbling she found the Ps and eventually what she sought. Over 40 Plumes were listed. Really, she thought releasing a long breath, shutting the tattered volume and putting it back on the top of the pile, I don't think I've ever been such a panicky fool before. She felt a sudden urge for the sovereign remedy for stress, a good hot cup of tea.

In the Brading train Gail deliverately applied the full force of her very considerable intelligence and innate honesty to the possibility, infinitesimal though it was, of

17

the Fenella Plume of the marriage certificate being John Morley's first wife and Richard's mother. She could have been a war widow, party to an impulsive immature marriage. If so, why was it never mentioned? She might not have wanted it known, and John Morley would undoubtedly have respected her wishes.

Gail shut her eyes and nerved herself to face a final catastrophic possibility. Suppose Fenella and Stephen Ash *had* married, discovered an absolutely impossible degree of incompatibility, and decided to part company for good without the formality of a divorce? In honesty one had to accept that this *was* a possibility.

She was aware of a sudden tenseness. Then suddenly the list of Plumes in the London telephone directory asserted itself. This damned masochism's got to stop, she told herself. Logically it was just possible that there had been no divorce, if that Fenella Plume had in fact been known later as Fenella Morley. But from the point of view of probability and horse sense it simply isn't on. All the same, I'll give a hostage to fortune by not saying a word about this afternoon at St Catherine's House to a living soul.

She relaxed. The train flashed through a station. To her surprise she realised that she was due at Brading in a quarter of an hour.

Richard was on the platform to meet her.

'Yes,' she said in answer to his enquiry, ' a good day. Everything I went up for is in the bag. How about the *Decameron*?'

'Pop and I have put in a whale of a day. I've come here straight from MBR. Quite a lot of torn and loose pages but only half a one actually missing. We'd planned to start on getting off the parchment and what's left of the original cover tomorrow, but Adrian rang at lunchtime to say he's coming down tomorrow for the night to celebrate the end of term, and of course he'll want to see the book as a whole.'

'Super about Adrian. He'll be home for Easter as well, won't he?'

'Sure. Wednesday to Tuesday, so he'll be here to help carry the can at Mum's party on Easter Monday. Back to Oxford on the Tuesday to pick up his traps and then off to Ephesus.'

'Being a successful don's a good life, isn't it?'

'Damn good. I know I haven't Adrian's grey matter. I've got a wife though.'

'Honours easy: I've got a husband. I suppose you haven't managed to get home all day? Poor old Gyp must have had a poorish time.'

'Rose promised to collect him when she took Tim for his walk, so he won't have done too badly, and I'm quite sure he'll have wheedled an extra meal out of Mrs Polts,' Richard said, referring to their daily help.

An exuberant welcome greeted them at the Dower House, and the estimable Mrs Polts had left a hot two-course meal in the slow oven. As they finished it Richard contemplated his wife.

'You look just about all in. Let's bung all these things into the dishwasher and go up early. I could do with a good night's sleep myself.'

Gail agreed, conscious for a fleeting moment of her earlier tension.

Shortly before midday on the following morning Adrian Morley drove through Buckford, having covered the distance from Oxford in record time. As he passed he glanced up at Morley's Book Restoration enveloped in weekend calm, and keenly anticipated inspecting the Mandeville *Decameron*. He returned the waves of several passersby, and pressed on to Glade Manor which still represented home to him.

John and Fenella Morley had decided to let him grow up aware of his adoption from infancy. The fact that they had 'chosen' him had been subtly emphasised from the first, and made understandable to him by learning that both his natural parents had been killed in a car disaster when he was a few months old. There had been occasional difficult psychological stages but his growing-up had been greatly helped by his much above-average intellectual ability. From the entrance to his preparatory school a succession of scholarships and academic successes had led to the Readership in Classical Archaeology which he now held at Athanasius College, Oxford.

John and Rose Morley were immensely proud of Adrian's achievements but disappointed by his apparent lack of interest in women.

'It's not as though he isn't run after,' John grumbled as they waited for his arrival. 'He's personable all right. He's got a future and is pulling down a tidy income already with his job and books and whatever. And you know what he's down for in my will if a bloody Labour government hasn't snitched the lot by then. And look at Richard and Gail,' he went on with rising indignation. 'It's their fifth wedding anniversary in the autumn and not a hint of a baby. Seems to me the Morleys are on the way out.'

Rose attempted reasoned consolation.

'Young people seem to want a bit of freedom before they finally commit themselves to the tie of a family these days. At least the saner ones do. Isn't that Adrian's car coming up the drive?'

A couple of short blasts on a horn confirmed the fact and they hurried to the front door.

Adrian was half a head shorter and more lightly built than John and Richard, and in contrast to their fairness had dark eyes and hair.

'Terrific to be back,' he said, kissing Rose and being slapped on the back by John. 'Are the others coming to lunch?'

He learnt that Richard and Gail were having a morning's golf but a family supper was being organised by Nanky.

'I'll just dash up to my room and dump my bag,' he said, 'and I'll be with you. Has Nanky got over her sister's death and the funeral and everything?'

He stopped to fondle Tim, an elderly retriever, a cherished family pet of long standing.

'Oh, absolutely,' Rose replied. 'It was a merciful release, as they say. The poor old thing was over 90 and only Nanky's half-sister anyway. Nanky said she felt she ought to go up to the funeral out of respect, but I honestly don't think there was any grief involved.'

'I'll drop in on her this afternoon and have a few words,' Adrian said as he ran up the stairs. 'You can bring me up to date on the Mandeville *Decameron* over lunch, Dad. I simply can't wait to see it.'

As a result of the absolute insistence of John and Rose, Nanky's activities in the house had been cut down when she reached pensionable age. Unless there were guests lunch was a simple meal cooked by one of a rota of daily women from the village. After gilding the lily as far as the housework was concerned Nanky retired to her flatlet until it was time to start preparations for dinner, the main meal of the day.

After lunch and further chat over coffee in the library Adrian went up to call on her. In token of being off duty she had discarded her white overall and was relaxing over the *Daily Mirror* in a comfortable chair by an electric fire. As he came in she looked up at him, her pleasure disguised by a look of critical appraisal.

She simply doesn't change a bit, Adrian thought. Still

21

the same round apple-cheeked face and those sharp blue eyes behind steel-rimmed spectacles. Hair just a shade whiter, perhaps ...

'So here you are,' she said. 'That end-of-term look about you I know well enough by now. Chasing all the way down here just for 24 hours. Pull up that chair.'

Adrain stooped to plant a smacking kiss on her barely wrinkled forehead and complied.

'Only a flying visit, it's true,' he said, 'but it just peps me up for the end-of-term jobs I've got to do before I come down for Easter.'

'Then you'll be off again for foreign parts I hear tell.'

'Yes. Ten days in Ephesus where exciting things are being dug up ... Nanky, I won't say that I was sorry to hear about your half-sister. She'd had a good long innings, hadn't she?'

'Ninety-two years and four months. I only hope I'm in my grave long before I get that far. And I didn't know her all that well, her being all that much older, but it seemed right and proper to go up to her funeral and sort out her bits of things. I took up an empty case just to bring a few bits and pieces back. The matron of the almshouses made me very welcome. I'll say that.'

They sat chatting for a short time and Adrian finally glanced at his watch.

'I must push off,' he said. 'Dad wants to run me over to the Works to see a famous old book that's come in to be mended. But when I'm down for Easter, Nanky, I'll take you out for a drive. We'll have lunch somewhere and you can point out all the things that are wrong with the cooking.'

'Cheeky you were as a little boy and cheeky you still are,' she replied, clearly gratified. 'But I won't say I shan't enjoy an outing with you.'

'Ok. That's a date then. See you this evening. I'm

looking forward to my dinner already, I can tell you.'

He gave her a hug and hurried off to spend an absorbing afternoon at Morley's Book Restoration with John, considering every feature of the Mandeville's *Decameron*.

In due course all five members of the family sat down to clear soup, duck, strawberries and cream and a special savoury invented by Nanky.

'No better meal than this ever came out of the College kitchen,' Adrian remarked.

'It's numbers,' Nanky commented cryptically. 'You just can't do the same. Now, Mrs Reckitt's here to help, so I don't want no one else in the kitchen. Coffee's waiting in the library in the thermos jugs.'

'A bottle of that Cognac I brought back from France last autumn's waiting too,' John Morley added.

In the library a wood fire flickered cheerfully on the hearth. The family party gathered round, well-fed and relaxed.

'Your Easter Monday party's on as usual, I take it, Mum?' Richard asked presently.

'Oh, yes,' Rose replied. 'Dare we hope for two fine Easter Mondays running I wonder? And that reminds me. The two young Crabbes have accepted, and undertaken to bring poor Henrietta Legge. I do hope she won't lose her nerve at the last minute. It's high time she started leading a normal social life again.'

'What exactly happened?' Adrian asked. 'I was having my year in the States and never caught up properly on it. I met her once or twice and thought her charming, but never really knew her.'

'It's a complicated story,' Gail said. 'She was engaged to Basil Railsdon of Loxford. He was simply rolling in money and the prospective Tory candidate for the Shirborough constituency. On the way back from his adoption meeting he was running late and took a short cut. A little girl fell out of a tree in front of his car and fractured her skull and died at once. He thought he would be blamed and lose his chance of the Shirborough seat, and managed to hide the body. I'm not absolutely clear about the next bit.'

'I am, more or less, I think,' John Morley took up. 'At the same time young Jeremy Crabbe whom you know, of course, managed to get a grave opened in Loxford church to disprove that the last Abbess but one of Loxford Abbey had been buried in it. Railsdon hid the body in the empty grave which was left partly open overnight and closed up the next morning. But just when he had apparently got away with it a piece of an earring the child was wearing was discovered embedded in a tyre of Railsdon's car. I can't remember the exact details, but Railsdon shot himself just as the police — Scotland Yard — had taken over the case, got the grave open again and the other earring was found on the child's body.'

'Good God! What a ghastly story,' Adrian exclaimed. 'No wonder Henrietta hasn't felt like going about.'

'There was another tragic love affair earlier on,' Rose said. 'I've just remembered. She was engaged to someone in one of the Guards regiments, and he was killed in a flying accident. And you know that Railsdon's daughter married Jeremy Crabbe. They are awfully good to her. They've bought a holiday cottage opposite hers and get down as often as they can.'

'Well, let's hope they can persuade her to come over on Easter Monday,' Gail commented. 'Not too obtrusive friendliness would be the best line to take, I should think.'

There was general concurrence, and the conversation turned to other topics.

'I noticed Russell's, the estate agent's, car outside

Hob's Cottage when we went over to MBR this afternoon,' John Morley remarked presently. 'They seem to be having trouble in selling the place.'

'It wants quite a bit spending on it,' Richard said. 'The roof's in a poorish way to start with. What sort of a neighbour do we want? Companionable, or a competent gardener who'd put in a bit of time for both of us?'

'It depends on the degree of companionability, if there is such a word,' Gail suggested. 'Anyway, it would be nice to have the place occupied again. There's always something a bit spooky about an uninhabited house.'

Chapter 3

Both at Glade Manor and the Dower House Sunday morning breakfast was an individual affair. Thanks to electric hot plates, bacon and eggs were available as required. When on duty as church-warden at Buckford parish church John Morley attended the mid-morning service, usually accompanied by Rose. Nanky cooked a robust Sunday lunch and was then off duty for the rest of the day, a friend from a nearby farm giving her a lift to Evensong. The church attendance of Richard and Gail was somewhat spasmodic.

On this particular Sunday Adrian woke early. As a drizzling rain was falling he abandoned the idea of the walk he had intended, rolled over and went to sleep again. He surfaced at 11, got up, and went to drop in on Richard and Gail before the Manor lunch. Finally he departed for Oxford in the afternoon.

After he had gone John Morley, who had numerous useful contacts in the world of valuable books, settled down to a round of telephoning. The final outcome of this exceeded his most optimistic expectations. By mid-evening he had established contact with the owner of another copy of the 1576 edition of the *Decameron*.

'Ours is in quite fair shape,' an elderly and decidedly uppercrust voice with a trace of Scots informed him, speaking from a stately home in the Border country. 'Of course we should be delighted for you or anyone from your well-known firm to come up and have a look at it ... Put you up with pleasure. We're a bit off the map here and enjoy having visitors from the outer world ... Your daughter-in-law? Spendid! Next Thursday would be perfectly all right by us ... All the better if the job takes several days!'

John finally put down the receiver, picking it up again after a couple of seconds and dialling the Dower House.

'I'm in touch with one Sir Ian Carstairs-Drummond,' he announced triumphantly. 'Believe it or not, he's got a copy of the *Decameron* of the same edition as Mandeville's. He lives in a remote part of the Borders, and will be delighted to welcome you on Thursday, Gail.'

'Here!' Richard interposed. 'Sending my wife off into the unknown like this. Who put you on to him?'

'Henley,' John Morley replied referring to the head librarian of a distinguished Cambridge college. 'There's a Lady Carstairs-Drummond, I gathered, eminent in the Girl Guide world. Gail simply must be the one to go. You and I hardly know a word of Italian.'

'Calm your fears, darling,' Gail adjured her husband. 'I foresee a severely academic and probably austere atmosphere with an emphasis on good works. Dare one hope for central heating, I wonder?'

On the following morning intensive work on Lord Mandeville's *Decameron* began at Morley's Book Restoration, involving some experienced members of the permanent staff as well as John, Richard and Gail. After the cautious removal of the case cover the threads of each section of the book were cut with extreme care and each page examined in detail. By Wednesday Gail had made full notes of every passage illegible as a result of stains and tearing, all of which she hoped to copy from the Carstairs-Drummond book, together with the missing half-page.

'Fortunate,' she remarked, 'that Italian was one of my A-level subjects. I expect some of Boccaccio's sixteenth-century phraseology will floor me, but Adrian ought to be able to rustle up somebody at Oxford who can help.'

It was decided that she should spend Wednesday night in London in order to catch an early train to Scotland the next morning. John Morley drove her into Brading in mid-afternoon. On his way home he slowed down as one of the vans of Frewley, a Brading builder, began to emerge from the gate of Hob's Cottage. The two vehicles drew up alongside.

'Afternoon, sir,' the driver said, whom John knew through contacts over building work on the Glade property. 'I expect you've met your new neighbour already. He's bought Hob's Cottage and we've been discussing jobs that want doing. Mr Stephen Ash, sir. Mr Morley of Glade Manor up there in the trees, Mr Ash.'

'No, we haven't met up to now,' John replied, 'although I've noticed some comings and goings over here. Good afternoon, Mr Ash. Hope you'll like it down here.'

He registered a man of roughly his own age with an outdoor look and shrewd grey eyes.

'Thanks. This,' Stephen Ash gestured in the direction of Hob's Cottage, 'is just about what I've been looking around for.'

John Morley asked if he knew the neighbourhood, and the other laughed.

'I've been off the map so long that all the UK feels like foreign parts. I emigrated to Australia when I came out of the army and I've been there ever since. Things don't seem too rosy over here from all accounts, but I began to feel I'd like to end up in the Old Country come hell or high water.'

'Well, I hope we'll see something of you when you move in. I expect a fair amount wants doing at Hob's. You've picked the right building firm, though.'

'Reckon I have. I'm hoping to muscle in a bit myself, though. I was in the construction line down under. I ... '

A hoot from an approaching car broke up the conversation and Frewley's can drove off in the direction of Buckford. Back at Glade Manor John Morley reported the encounter to his wife.

'Quite a decent chap, I thought,' he said. 'Not on our wave-length but reasonably presentable for an occasional drinks party.'

'We might ask him to the Easter Monday do,' Rose suggested.

'That's a thought. He'd pass in a crowd all right.'

When encountered in Buckford a few days later Stephen Ash seemed genuinely pleased at the invitation but regretted that although he hardly knew a soul in the UK, he had got a date for Easter Monday.

'Don't tell me,' John said. 'The race meeting over at Westingham.'

'You've got me in one, Mr Morley. After all my years down under I just can't keep away from the gees, and fixed up to go with a bloke I met in a pub while I was house-hunting.'

'It's a good meeting. Hope you enjoy it and back some winners. Plenty of time to come along up to us!'

When John Morley reported that Stephen Ash had declined the invitation as he already had a date for Easter Monday, Rose remarked that it was probably a good thing.

'A bit daunting for him to be plunged into a house

full of total strangers who all know themselves well and are old friends of ours. And Ash doesn't seem to be going down all that well locally. Not with the local people and such anyway.'

'Which of them?' her husband asked.

'Well, I was in Little's yesterday and he seems to have had a breeze with them over some paint he'd ordered. Bob Little ended by telling him that he could take his custom somewhere else. And apparently when our Maggie Head took the trouble to get off her bike the other day to shut the Hob's Cottage gate which was swinging in the wind he burst out and told her to mind her own bloody business.'

'Bit of luck that it's the Westingham races, then. We'll ask him up alone sometime and rope in Richard and Gail.'

The days following Gail's departure for Scotland were busy but uneventful. At Morley's Book Restoration work on the *Decameron* went on steadily: the cautious cleaning of stains, the repairing of torn pages and the dicey problem of restoring the mutilated cover. At Glade Manor, Rose and Nanky discussed the menu for the Easter Monday informal lunch, and extra stores were ordered. From time to time there were signs of activity at Hob's Cottage — Stephen Ash's Fiesta, Frewley's vans and a delivery van from a Brading furniture store. Telephone calls from Gail announced highly enjoyable surroundings and warm hospitality on the part of her elderly host and hostess. She reported good progress in the collecting of missing data needed to fill the gaps in the Mandeville copy of the *Decameron*. She would be back on the Thursday evening before Easter.

Adrian heralded the Easter reunion at Glade by arriving on the previous evening. The next day he fulfilled

30

his promise to Nanky by taking her out to lunch at a not too overpowering hotel at Craythorne Bay, 12 miles from Buckford. It was a highly successful outing. Reminiscence played a large part in the conversation, Adrian marvelling at Nanky's recollection of incidents in his childhood and adolescence which he himself had forgotten. The hotel lunch in general met with her approval apart from the consistency of the Yorkshire pudding served with the roast beef.

'Properly leathery,' she commented. 'Not beaten up proper.'

On the way home they touched on Fenella Morley's death and the comfort that Rose had brought into John Morley's shattered life.

'And if you'd told me I could ever work with a new mistress in Glade Manor I'd never've believed you,' Nanky avowed.

After a silence she turned and looked intently at Adrian.

'Tis time you found yourself a wife,' she said.

'Well, Nanky,' he replied, 'you're not much of a one to preach about holy matrimony, are you?'

'Reckon I found a ready-made family,' she said. 'You're past 30, Adrian. Time you gave your mind to it. There's more to life than books and digging up things hundreds of years old in foreign parts.'

Adrian laughed.

'Well, you old matchmaker,' he said, 'if ever I get round to popping the question you shall be the first to hear about it.'

Late that evening Gail returned, full of praise for the kindness of the Carstairs-Drummonds, and of satisfaction at the gaps in the text of the Mandeville *Decameron* that she was now able to fill. John Morley was particularly delighted by the colour photographs of the cover which she had taken.

'Red, right enough,' he exclaimed. 'This is more than I dared hope for.'

Breakfast on the following morning at the Dower House was later and more leisurely than usual. As Gail listened to Richard's catalogue of items of local news she suddenly decided that she could no longer keep to herself the news that had by now become a reasonable certainty.

'Oh, by the way,' Richard said before she could speak, 'a chap's bought Hob's Cottage. Ash, he's called. Stephen Ash.'

She could feel her surroundings blacking out as she slipped from her chair to the floor.

The darkness swirled and finally cleared to reveal Richard's horror-struck face as he bent over her. His arms were round her, raising her from the kitchen floor.

'I'm perfectly all right, darling,' she heard a travesty of her own voice saying. As she spoke life resolved itself into a gigantic question mark. Was she to tell him what she had heard in St Catherine's House, or not . . .? Now . . . ?

In the event Richard supplied the answer.

'Gail — darling — is it? Can it possibly be . . .?'

She looked up into his eyes, and replied with perfect, if partial truth.

'I really think so, dearest. Two consecutive blanks.'

'We'll get Greaves. Now — right away. He might be out on his rounds — anyway, they can track him down. Lie still.'

Gail listened to Richard's running footsteps on the stairs. Lying on her bed she had the sensation of being in a curious double-layered dream. Uppermost was the almost unbelievable possibility of the pregnancy so long hoped for. But below this was the sinister arriᵛal on the Morley doorstep, so to speak, of the man who had obviously come to use the knowledge he possessed to shatter the happiness of the people who meant most to her in the world. What, if anything, ought she to do?

She pressed the palms of her hands to her temples in the effort to think clearly. Nothing, she felt, was likely to happen over Easter. Stephen Ash had plenty of time at his disposal. He would get himself established at Hob's Cottage before embarking on his programme of — almost certainly — blackmail. On Easter Monday there was Rose's annual alfresco lunch party, and on the following day Rose and John, together with Richard and herself, were driving down to that wedding in Cornwall, and not returning until the Thursday. That gave one time to think.

The sound of a car drawing up at the front door could mean Dr Greaves. Gail braced herself to appear normal and sensible. A few minutes later Richard brought him into the room, gave her the V-sign and withdrew. Dr Greaves, who had succeeded his father in the practice and was an old friend of the Morleys, greeted her cheerfully as the door closed.

'Now, my dear, what's all this in aid of, I wonder?' he asked, sitting down on the edge of the bed.

Gail began to talk, calmly and sensibly ... there was plenty of relevant matter unconnected with Stephen Ash, she told herself. Dr Greaves listened attentively, and asked her a number of questions.

Later, as he finished his examination, he began to whistle a tune softly. Gail's heart gave a sudden leap as she looked up at him.

'I see you are Gilbert & Sullivan addict like me,' he said. '*No possible doubt whatever*'. He went to the door and called Richard. 'Keep her in bed for the rest of the day and she'll be as right as rain, if you don't let her work too hard at William the Conqueror's diary or

33

whatever it is you're all so hooked on at the Works.'

After he had gone the rest of the day seemed to Gail to have a dreamlike quality. While aware that the week or so ahead was only a brief respite from the Stephen Ash threat she seemed able to relax. After Dr Greaves had gone there was an unforgettable half-hour with Richard. There followed at intervals John Morley, triumphant, and Rose, her delight just tinctured with anxiety about Gail's welfare.

'You simply mustn't do too much, darling,' she said. 'At Monday's party, especially. Just fade out unobtrusively if you feel yourself getting tired.'

Adrian announced himself intrigued at the thought of becoming an uncle.

'Why is it' he asked, 'that the adjective that springs to the lips is "wicked"? Think of the little Princes in the Tower and any number of situations like that. I shall of course be the shining exception.'

Nanky installed herself in the Dower House kitchen and prepared a lunch and supper that she considered suitable for an expectant mother. After the mild sedative left by Dr Greaves Gail slept well, waking rested and restored, and able to view the uncertainties of the near future calmly. She recognised in herself a curious feeling that something would happen which would of itself decide her own course of action.

On getting out of bed on Easter Monday morning John Morley pulled back the curtains and surveyed the heavens.

'Definite improvement on last night,' he remarked to Rose. 'Cumulus clouds bowling along and quite a bit of blue sky. With any luck it should be OK by the time people start turning up.'

An Easter Monday informal lunch party had been a

34

tradition during Fenella Morley's time and Rose had carried it on. After a hasty breakfast the inmates of both the Manor and the Dower House took up the familiar routine without delay. The weather was improving steadily, and John and Richard set out garden seats and deck chairs in sheltered spots before beginning on the installation of a bar in the spacious front hall. Appetising odours crept through from the kitchen premises. Here, under Nanky's supervision, daily women from Buckford tempted by treble pay for bank holiday work were producing a variety of fresh appetising snacks. As these arrived in relays on trays Rose and Gail arranged them to advantage on long tables in the hall and library. Supplies of hot soup and coffee were organised.

At midday sounds of the first arrivals' cars were audible and Adrian hurried off to arrange parking in both the Manor and the Dower House drives.

At a quarter past twelve he was acclaimed by Jeremy and Amanda Crabbe as they drew up in their car.

'Park prettily, please,' Adrian adjured Jeremy. 'Where do you think you are? Back at Athanasius?'

He went round to open the passenger doors, noting that Henrietta Legge had not panicked at the last moment. Amanda, sitting in front with her husband, turned round in her seat to introduce Adrian. He got an impression of well-cut features, pallor and overall control, and embarked on a reference to their meeting some years earlier. This was cut short by the arrival of another car.

'Sorry you've got to walk a bit,' he said. 'First arrivals have appropriated the drive in front of the house.'

'We can just about make it, I think,' Amanda replied. 'Come on, both of you.'

The trio set off with Henrietta Legge between them. In the spacious hall of Glade House drinks were in full swing and immediately pressed on the Crabbes and Henrietta. The catastrophe of Basil Railsdon's suicide and the subsequent scandal had aroused much sympathy for her, and to the Crabbes' relief she had no lack of people to chat to. Gradually they allowed themselves to become involved with their own friends.

As always the Easter Monday party was being highly successful. Guests formed and reformed small groups, wandering from the hall to the drawing room and library. The hardier of them went out into the garden and appropriated the seats in sheltered sunny spots. The Morleys moved from group to group, renewing contacts and exchanging news. Adrian came upon a hilarious party of younger guests which included the Crabbes. He asked how Henrietta was getting on.

'Fine, I think,' Amanda said. 'I saw her just now going down to have a look at the rock garden. She's made a tiny one of her own and is rather sold on rock plants.'

The Manor rock garden was reached by a flight of stone steps leading down from the gently sloping flower garden in front of the house. Adrian found several groups of rock plant enthusiasts engaged in detailed scrutinies and earnest conversation. After a few words with these he had a sudden impulse to take the rough narrow path down to the stepping stones across the Weaving. It was as the little river glinted through the trees that he saw Henrietta. She was sitting alone on a fallen tree trunk, apparently gazing at the water.

'You've beaten me to it,' he said, sitting down on the tree trunk himself. 'I often nip down here for a breather when we've got something on. Rather a good spot, isn't it?'

'Delightful,' Henrietta replied while barely turning her head. 'Such lovely reflections in the water. Does the cottage over there belong to you, too?'

'No, it doesn't. The river's the boundary of the Glade property on this side. A chap called Ash has just bought it and is doing quite a bit in the way of improvements, apparently. It's old. Some sixteenth-century bits, actually. Would you like to go over and have a look? I happen to know that the new owner's gone off to the Westingham races.'

'Yes, I'd like to, if you think he wouldn't mind.'

'I'm sure he wouldn't. The stream's so low at the moment that the stepping stones are no problem.'

They crossed the Weaving and went up a couple of grassy steps on the far side. Ladders, sacks of cement and a variety of building equipment were in evidence. Adrian pointed out early features of interest: the big external chimney, the obvious addition at a later period of an upper storey showing a slight overhang, and some rough stone carving over the front door of black oak.

'Stephen Ash, the chap who's bought the place, went out to Australia when he was demobbed after the war,' he said, in an attempt to keep a normal flow of conversation going. 'He's been there ever since but began to get a yen to spend his declining years in the Old Country. He's been looking around and finally decided that this was just what he wanted and could afford.'

Henrietta showed polite interest, but Adrian sensed a deep unhappiness. No stimulus or satisfying purpose in her life after that awful mess-up. Just going on existing.

They negotiated the stepping stones and returned to the Manor grounds.

'I'll lead the way up,' he said. 'Just watch your feet a bit. Some of the stones on the path are getting loose. I must remember to tell Dad. It's important to keep the place in a decent shape. I must tell you our good news. Gail, my brother Richard's wife, has started a baby at long last, so we must look ahead where the estate's concerned. Let's hope it's a boy.'

A moment or so later he was suddenly conscious that Henrietta was no longer just behind him and the sound of her steps had suddenly stopped. He swung round to see her leaning against a tree trunk, her body shaken with sobs.

'There's a seat a few yards ahead,' he said quietly. With his arm firmly round her shoulders he propelled her towards it.

In a few moments she had herself in hand and was drying her eyes.

'I do apologise,' she said shakily. 'What an appalling way to behave. It ... it just came over me that there's absolutely nothing in life for me to look ahead to, and looking back is just plain hell.'

Adrain was silent for a brief space, recognising that anything in the nature of facile reassurances would be worse than useless.

'Did you feel wholly satisfied with the prospect of life ahead as Basil Railsdon's wife?' he asked at last.

Henrietta raised her head and their eyes met.

'No,' she said. 'He offered me a lot, of course: money, status and recognised identity. The alternative was an increasingly restricted life. And an increasingly isolated one. You must have seen it happen. A rather badly-off unmarried woman without an interesting career becomes a dropout. I wasn't in love with him.'

There was a distant sound of a car starting up.

'Hell!' Adrian exclaimed, astonishing himself with his vehemence. 'People are beginning to go. I'll have to go and be a car park attendant, I suppose.'

They both got to their feet and began to walk up the path.

38

'Thank you, Henrietta,' he said, 'for talking to me as you just have.'

'And thank you for listening in the way you did,' she answered in a low voice. She paused for a split second and he saw her right hand go up to her right ear.

'You've lost an earring,' he said, conscious that an opportunity had presented itself. 'I'll go over the ground and have a look when everybody's cleared off.'

Disregarding her protests he escorted her to the gravel sweep in front of the house where departing guests were beginning to gather. It was nearly 4 o'clock when the last car-load disappeared down the drive.

The Morleys stopped waving, turned and went into the house with unconcealed signs of exhaustion. As they sank into chairs in the hall Nanky appeared propelling a tea trolley.

'Thought they'd never go, that last lot,' she remarked concisely, parking the trolley in front of Rose. 'Nice hot cuppas are what you all want.'

The Morleys assured her in their different idioms that she was bang on, as Richard put it.

'Really strong for me, please Mum,' he said. 'And three lumps.'

As they revived they reviewed the day, agreeing that it had been a particularly successful Easter Monday lunch picnic.

'Enormous luck over the weather,' John remarked. 'Let's hope it holds for the drive tomorrow. What time had we better start?'

After some discussion, 10.30 was agreed upon. John, Rose, Richard and Gail were due at a wedding in Cornwall on Wednesday, preceded by a party on the Tuesday evening.

'I'll have to push off early, too,' Adrian said. 'There

39

were a few things I didn't get round to before I came down.'

'What time's your plane on Thursday?' Gail asked.

'The ungodly hour of 8.30 a.m. at Heathrow.'

'I strongly recommend an early night for everybody, then,' Rose said. 'Nanky included. I thought she was looking decidedly tired when she brought this tea in. I feel restored, and I'm going to put a few things together for tomorrow.'

The family dispersed. Adrian went up to his room and sat deep in thought for some minutes. He then slipped unobtrusively downstairs and out into the garden by a side door. Cutting through the rock garden, his eyes searching the ground as he went, he took the path through the trees down to the river. He had a memory retentive of detail. As he had steered Henrietta towards the wooden seat on realising that she was weeping, there had been a projecting low branch on the right of the path. He remembered trying to draw her away from it. He located the exact spot, dropped on to his knees and began to search among the twigs and dead leaves. Unbelievably something glinted. The next moment he was looking down at the small crystal and sapphire earring in the palm of his hand. He stared at it, incredulous at his luck. If I ever go to Padua, he thought, I'll do something really handsome in the way of lighting candles or whatever one does in honour of St Anthony.

No one was about when he returned to the house, and he decided to put through a call to Henrietta at once. Her voice when it came over the line was instantly recognisable.

'Adrian Morley here,' he said, hoping that his own voice sounded normal. 'Just to let you know that I've found your earring. It was on the path, near the seat. I'll

40

drop it in on my way back to Oxford tomorrow morning. Would about half past ten be all right?'

'Of course. Any time. But won't it be bringing you out of your way. It's bound to. I mean, there's absolutely no hurry ...'

Her voice was a little breathless as if she were both astonished and diffident.

'No problem in the world,' he said. 'I'll be along then, plus earring. Good night.'

He put down the receiver and returned to his room, trying to analyse what had happened to him in the space of about six hours.

Chapter 4

After a hasty breakfast on the following morning Adrian went out to the kitchen to say goodbye to Nanky. He found her upstairs in the sitting room of her flatlet.

'Hallo!' he said. 'I've just looked in to say goodbye. I hope you aren't too whacked after yesterday?'

'Stuff and nonsense,' she retorted. 'A busy day I'll grant you, but everything ran smooth as silk. Now when you're all out from under my feet I'm going on sorting my sister's things in peace and quiet.' As she spoke she indicated a battered suitcase on a chair. 'Don't you forget now that you promised to send me a postcard.'

'I won't,' he said. 'I might even make it two. And I'm due back in England on Saturday week, and might manage to pop down for a night before term starts.'

He gave her a hug and a smacking kiss and hurried off with a final wave from the door. Rose was right. Nanky did look a bit fagged.

John and Rose had come down and were just starting their breakfast in the dining-room.

'I'm off,' he said. 'I hope you have a good run and decent champagne at the wedding breakfast.'

'And you a good flight, darling,' Rose said. 'Is there any chance of your getting down again before term starts?'

'With a spot of luck. I'll ring from College as soon as I get back. You could always contact me c/o International Excavations, Ephesus.'

'Fine,' John Morley said. 'By that time we ought to have got the *Decameron* into something like shape. Have a good trip, old man.'

Within a few minutes Adrian was coasting down the drive, giving a series of toots as he passed the turning to the Dower House.

Once clear of Buckford, and out on the familiar road to Oxford which he would follow for the next forty miles before diverging to Loxford, his thoughts reverted to Henrietta Legge and his astonishing reaction to her. There had been a few shortlived affairs in his life but this was in a totally different category. Did love at first sight accompanied by a sense of overwhelming certainty actually happen outside romantic novels, he asked himself? He went over the events of the previous afternoon with a scholar's accuracy. Was there anything, however slight, to suggest for one single moment that Henrietta had, in the midst of her distress, fallen for him? An honest thinker, he admitted to himself that there had not. One thing was absolutley vital: he must not attempt to rush matters. A woman of her type needed time to get over a really appalling shock.

In spite of this reasoned conclusion he found himself picturing married life with Henrietta ... an Oxford house, not too far from Athanasius ... talking over the day's events ... attending public functions with her at his side drawing admiring glances ... holidays .... He made a determined effort to pull himself together and think more analytically. The academic distinction that he had already acquired had been his defence against an underlying sense of inferiority at being an adopted child in however loving and caring a home. With Henrietta he could found a home in his own right for his own children. Presently he was jolted into the present by a road sign announcing 'LOXFORD 4 1/2 miles'. On reaching the outskirts of the village he slowed down to ask a woman with a shopping basket the way to Miss Legge's house.

'Straight on and take the second turning on your left,' he was told. 'Two cottages up to the top and hers is on the left. You can't miss it.'

Adrian thanked her while aware of being eyed with keen interest. He drove on and negotiated the sharp turn into a rather narrow side road with caution, aware that his mind had become a complete blank. As he drew up at the gate of the cottage on the left his vision of a conversation *à deux* with Henrietta abruptly disintegrated into thin air. Jeremy Crabbe in slacks and an open-necked shirt materialised at the gate of the cottage opposite, and greeted him with a shout.

'Oyez! Enter knight-errant bearing missing jewel!'

'Fool!' Adrian replied, cursing under his breath, his mind instantly forming a decision ... he'd pack overnight ... As he got out of his car the front doors of both cottages opened and Henrietta and Amanda emerged.

'Madam,' he said, and handed Henrietta a match box with a smile. 'My apologies for the container. Quite beneath the dignity of the contents but the best I could rustle up.'

As she thanked him their eyes met and he fancied that he saw something more than pleasure at the recovery of a lost possession in hers. Or was it just wishful thinking on his part? Meanwhile the Crabbes were loudly demanding an account of the finding of the earring, and Henrietta made the inevitable gesture of inviting everyone into her cottage for coffee.

'We're off today, too,' Jeremy said at a later stage in

44

the conversation. 'Not until after tea, though. What time's your flight?'

'8.30 a.m. on Thursday,' Adrian told him.

'God! Must they?'

'I suppose the skies get congested at reasonable hours. Back on Saturday week. Meanwhile I'd better be moving on.'

Henrietta escorted him to the gate.

'I simply can't thank you enough,' she said as Adrian got in the driving seat.

'Nor I you,' he replied without looking at her, turning the key to start the engine and beginning to back down the lane. In the driving mirror he caught a glimpse of her standing at the gate before turning back into her cottage.

Adrian rang Nanky from Athanasius in the early evening.

'Nothing's wrong,' he assured her, 'except that I've been fool enough to leave behind some papers that I simply must take with me to Ephesus. I'll turn up about 10 tomorrow morning and pick them up.'

Nanky tut-tutted, said that it wasn't like him not to pack properly, and offered to put the papers into the post.

'No go,' Adrian explained. 'My plane takes off at 8.30 on Thursday morning which means that I've got to be at Heathrow by 7.30 at the latest. And if you posted them to me at Ephesus I'd be home again before they turned up there.'

'Not that I won't be glad to have another sight of you,' she conceded. 'And there'll be a good hot cup of coffee waiting.'

'Fine. Be seeing you early tomorrow. Goodbye for now, then.'

He rang off and began to collect up minimum

requirements for his trip to Ephesus, thinking rapidly as he did so. Say he got down to Glade by roughly half-past nine and stayed about an hour. If he knew anything of Nanky there would be something more than a good hot cup of coffee waiting for him. He would make Loxford by about half-past twelve. If the worst happened and Henrietta was out he would put a brief note through her letter box and go on the Heathrow. Fill in time up there, somehow. And if she was at home, what was he going to say to her? Wouldn't the fact that he had reappeared within 24 hours make some sort of an attempt at an explanation inevitable?

He was no nearer a decision on the matter when a pre-arranged ring from the porters' lodge woke him at 6 o'clock on the following morning. He left Oxford ahead of schedule, still incredulous at the step he was on the verge of taking. Traffic at this early hour was relatively light, and he drew up at the front door of Glade Manor at a quarter past nine. Nanky came hurrying out.

'Bless my soul!' she exclaimed. 'I didn't think to see you much before 10. Your breakfast isn't even on.'

'No problem,' Adrian assured her. 'In fact, all the better. I'll take old Tim up to the top to stretch my legs after the drive.'

Adapting his pace to the elderly retriever's he set off through the woods behind the house. They had been a fundamental part of his happy childhood: the scene of innumerable imaginary adventures. Under the pale blue spring sky something of their early spell reasserted itself. The sheer beauty of fresh green, the clumps of starry anemones and primroses and the hint of bluebells to come merged with his thoughts of Henrietta.

Presently they came to the crest of the ridge overlooking a disused quarry. Tim flopped down gratefully, panting a little. Adrian stood gazing down at the dip in the hills sheltering Glade Manor. A tractor was crawling up and down a slope of bare red earth, the faint drone of its engine just audible. In another field a man with a couple of dogs rounded up sheep. Glancing at his watch he decided that it was time to start down to Nanky and breakfast and patted Tim's head.

'Come on, old chap,' he said. 'Biscuit!'

On returning to the house he was confronted with a plate of bacon, eggs, sausages and tomatoes. He would have preferred to eat in the kitchen but Nanky had very definite ideas about what was proper, and a place had been laid for him at the dining-room table. She did, however, consent to sit and talk to him while he ate. He learnt that the family had got off pretty well on time on the previous morning. Mr and Mrs Richard would be returning late tonight, she told him, so that Mr Richard could get to the Works first thing tomorrow as there was an important book on hand. Mr and Mrs Morley were taking it a bit easier and would be back around tea time tomorrow. Adrian was relieved to find that she was vague about his own programme, apparently not clear as to whether he was going straight to Heathrow or returning to Oxford first.

She certainly was looking a bit under the weather, he thought, as he ate. Rose had been quite right.

'Where's your back-up staff?' he asked as he moved on to toast and marmalade. 'Mrs Reckitt and Co?'

'Couple o' days off, seeing as they worked bank holiday Monday,' Nanky replied. 'They finished clearing the place up yesterday after you'd all gone off, and they'll be back as usual Friday.'

The conversation turned to the wonderful news of Mrs Richard's baby.

'Better late than never,' Nanky announced oracularly, giving Adrian a meaning look.

'Well,' he said. 'I'd better be off, I suppose, when I've been up to my room to collect those papers. This super breakfast will see me through to Ephesus, I should think. Now ease up a bit, with everybody out of the house for once.'

Outside the front door he kissed her affectionately and got into his car. As he came to the curve in the drive he slowed to give her a final wave as she stood on the Manor steps, holding Tim by the collar.

While driving to Loxford Adrian formulated and rehearsed a number of opening phrases, none of which seemed to strike the right note. He arrived at the gate of Henrietta's cottage to find himself starkly confronted by an open, empty garage. The ground floor windows of the cottage were shut and locked. He looked at his watch. It was a quarter to one. Obviously she was out to lunch.

Having decided that 1 o'clock would irrevocably clinch matters he sat in his car and waited. Finally he tore a page from the blank sheets at the end of his pocket diary.

'I appear to have struck unlucky again,' he wrote. 'you must be lunching out somewhere. I'll ring you from Ephesus. Adrian.'

Rather to his surprise he found himself feeling that after all, things had turned out to his advantage. One could be reasonably certain no one had ever rung Henrietta from Ephesus before. He headed for Heathrow, booked in at one of the relatively modest hotels, and devoted most of the evening to trying to concentrate on the archaeological notes he had made on the dig in progress.

The Morleys returned to Glade in two instalments. Richard and Gail left soon after the departure of the bride and bridegroom, and arrived at the Dower House in the evening. They found a note left by their daily woman reporting all well and Gyp good as gold. She would bring him back next morning, and there was a hot snack simmering in the oven. The both slept soundly and Richard went off after breakfast to put in his usual day's work at Morley's Book Restoration. Gail devoted the morning to domestic matters in the intervals of giving Mrs Polts a detailed account of the wedding, including the clothes worn by the chief participants. In view of Richard's return to work John Morley had decided to take another day off and give Rose a brief break. They spent a night at a small hotel on their homeward route, and enjoyed a coastal walk on the Thursday morning. It was nearly 4 o'clock when they drove through Buckford on their way back.

'Good for Richard to be running the ship,' John remarked as they passed the turning to Morley's Book Restoration. 'I wonder how much headway's been made with Mandeville's *Decameron*?

Buckford slipped behind them. There was no one about in the purlieus of Hob's Cottage, and in a matter of moments they drove through the Manor gates and up the drive, and drew up at the front door.

They were confronted by a sight which for a moment reduced them both to speechlessness. The letter box was jammed open with a copy of *The Times* and some large envelopes. Rose grasped her husband's arm without speaking.

'Nanky's been taken ill from the look of it,' John Morley said abruptly, getting out of the car and feeling for his keys. A few moments later he had unlocked the front door and stepped over a litter of envelopes on the mat inside. The hall was silent and appeared exactly as usual. So did the kitchen premises. Joined by Rose he hurried up the stairs to Nanky's flatlet. Here, too,

49

everything was in perfect order. Rose flung open the hanging cupboard and quickly checked its contents.

'Her everyday coat's missing,' she said. 'The one she slips on for going out into the garden or walking Tim. And where *is* Tim?'

'God knows,' John replied, his brow corrugated by an anxious frown. 'Better go over the whole house.'

They inspected every room and looked into all cupboards and wardrobes without result. Finally they returned to the hall. John wrenched the newspaper out of the letter box.

'Today's,' he said, glancing at it. 'It's beginning to look like a coronary or something of the sort while she was out with Tim yesterday. Look, I'm going to ring the Works and get Richard back here at once. We'll do a quick search of the woods on the way up to the top. That's where she always took Tim. Get yourself a brandy, Rose, and go and sit down.'

A few minutes later he joined her in the library.

'Richard's coming over at once,' he said. 'I think' — he broke off at the sound of footsteps in the hall and they turned eagerly to the open door to see Gail raising a hand in welcome, and smiling.

'I heard the car,' she said, 'and felt I must pop over for a moment just to ... Something's wrong. What is it?'

'Darling, come and sit down,' Rose begged. 'We're worried. We've come back to find that Nanky's — well, disappeared. Since Wednesday some time from the look of it.'

As Gail sat down beside her and took her hand, a car came up the drive at speed and braked outside. Within seconds Richard was in the library.

'What's up?' he demanded.

John summed up the situation. He suddenly looked years older, Gail thought, thankful for Richard's arrival

50

and immediate assumption of responsibility.

'Obviously, Dad,' the latter was saying, 'the first thing is for us to go up to the top of the woods. That's where she always takes Tim for a walk . . . It's damned odd that he's missing, too. You two will be all right here, won't you?' he said, turning to his wife.

'Perfectly,' Gail replied, glancing at Rose who was still looking very shaken. 'I'll rustle up some sort of meal. One's got to eat, come hell and high water.'

The two men hurried off.

'We'll start off with a cuppa, Rose,' Gail said. 'It'll only take a few minutes.'

In Nanky's meticulously neat kitchen she busied herself with an electric kettle and teatray, her mind moving at speed. A ghastly idea, but what must have happened was that Nanky had taken Tim for his usual walk up to the top of the woods and had a coronary or a stroke or something, and just collapsed. Please God she'd died at once and not been lying there all this time, not able to make anybody hear. But what about Tim? Why hadn't he come home and tried to get in? She puzzled over his absence as she heated the teapot, and decided not to raise the subject with Rose.

The tea did them both good, and some colour returned to Rose's cheeks.

'Gail dear,' she said, 'I feel quite dreadful at you being mixed up in this with a baby on the way.'

'My dear Rose, I'm as fit as a fiddle. Doctor Greaves says so. And of course, fond of Nanky as I've always been, she doesn't mean quite as much to me as the family proper.'

'That's true of course,' Rose agreed, 'but all the same it's been a shock for you, too. I wonder if there's any hope at all of her being still alive?'

'Doubtful, I'm afraid . . . Look, hadn't we better

make a few plans for temporary domestic arrangements? Do you think you can get your various dailies to put in a bit of extra time for the moment?'

They were still discussing provisional arrangements when footsteps were audible and John and Richard Morley came into the library with impassive faces.

'She's almost at the bottom of the quarry slope,' John said, 'caught up in a clump of gorse. Tim's lying near her. I'm going to ring the police station over at Brading.'

He disappeared in the direction of his study. Richard thankfully gulped down a cup of tea.

'Look,' he said to Rose and Gail, 'we're all in this up to the neck and had better face facts. There are pretty clear signs that Nanky didn't just slip over the edge accidentally.'

They stared at him, aghast and speechless.

'You can't mean . . .?' Gail began, and broke off.

'Yes, I do,' Richard went on. 'It's where the track along the top of the ridge curves in a bit to keep clear of the bushes along the edge of the quarry. You know where I mean. Well, there's a bit where the bushes have been recently broken, and some footprints where the ground's a bit muddy. We thought we'd better keep clear of them, but it was easy to see poor old Tim's. He'd dug his claws in when he was dragged to the edge. We went along a bit and looked down. You can see them both, lying at the bottom of the quarry.'

The two women were still speechless with horror. John Morley's footsteps were audible as he came across the hall from his study and into the library, his face set.

'I got on to the police station at Brading,' he said. 'They're coming straight over.'

Gail felt a sudden urge to action. Anything was better than just sitting.

We've got to eat,' she said. 'May I invade the kitchen,

52

Rose? I'll go and get something organised for supper.'

'I'll come with you.' Rose followed her out of the room. The two men sat on, at intervals exchanging brief remarks about various aspects of the situation in which the family had suddenly found itself involved.

In under half an hour two police cars came up the drive. They parked outside the front door, and Detective Inspector Bosworth emerged from the leading one. John Morley who knew him slightly went out to meet him. They shook hands.

'I'm extremely sorry that you've come home to a situation like this, sir,' the Inspector said. 'I think the first step is for you and the other members of the family involved to give me a brief account of your movements over the past few days.'

'Right,' John said. 'Come along to the library.'

Glancing over his shoulder and giving his constable a nod to follow on, Inspector Bosworth accompanied John Morley across the hall. Richard had summoned Rose and Gail from the kitchen and there were brief introductions.

'To start off with, sir,' Inspector Bosworth said, 'I understand that all of you here present went away to a wedding on Tuesday morning leaving Miss Gover in charge here, while the Dower House was unoccupied?'

'That is correct,' John Morley replied.

'And you and your wife returned first, getting back to the Dower House last Wednesday evening, I believe, Mr Richard Morley?'

'Yes, I was due at the works in Buckford this morning.'

'What time did you get back here on Wednesday evening?'

'Just on a quarter past seven.'

'Thank you all for making everything very clear up to this point,' Inspector Bosworth said. 'What I'm going to

53

do now is to send Sergeant Maxwell and his support down to the quarry to investigate things there. I shall follow on when I've been up to the top here and seen what Mr Richard Morley has reported. I'd be glad if you'd come with me, sir. And I suggest Mr Morley stays here with the ladies. They've had a most unpleasant shock and I shouldn't like to leave them on their own just at present.'

'Thank you, Inspector,' John said. 'I certainly shouldn't either.'

About half an hour later Inspector Bosworth returned with Richard, and asked for the use of the telephone. With a good fire on the library hearth and a welcome smell of cooking coming from the kitchen there was some relaxation of tension.

'Decent chap, Bosworth,' Richard said, rubbing his cold hands. 'He's left the unfortunate bobby up at the top to see nothing's tampered with, but they'll send out a relief later. Meanwhile they're — well, coping with the situation down in the quarry.'

The distant tinkle of the telephone bell signalled the end of Inspector Bosworth's calls, and he returned to the library.

'Now, sir,' he said addressing John Morley, 'we can leave you in peace tonight, except that you'll hear the relief for the chap I've posted up top coming in a police car. As soon as it's properly light tomorrow I'll be sending photographers up, and I'll be in touch with you. There's just one more question: has anyone been in Miss Gover's room since you and Mrs Morley returned this evening?'

'My wife and I went in when we were searching the house. No one else has, to my knowledge.' He glanced at Gail and Richard who shook their heads.

'You'll understand, I'm sure, sure, sir, that we must

lock up the room and keep the key until we have searched it tomorrow. Miss Gover might have received a letter arranging a meeting up by the quarry.'

'Good God, I never thought of that,' John Morley said. 'Of course. Come up to her flat and we'll lock it, and you can take the key.'

There was a good deal of coming and going in the grounds of Glade Manor from first light on the following morning. John and Richard went off to the Works as usual, leaving a message for Inspector Bosworth to say that they were, of course, immediately available if required. Rose and Gail did their best to satisfy the appalled and avid curiosity of their daily women and get the normal domestic work of their respective houses carried out. In the early afternoon Inspector Bosworth called at the works to tell John that the inquest had been fixed for 10 o'clock on the following Monday morning, and would be held in the parish hall at Buckford.

'It'll be adjourned for a week in the first instance,' he said. 'The death certificate will be issued so that you can go ahead with funeral arrangements. Are there any relatives to be consulted?'

'None that we know of,' John Morley replied. 'There was a much older half-sister but she died recently.'

Inspector Bosworth glanced at his notebook.

'One other point, sir. I understand that your elder son, Mr Adrian Morley, was at Glade Manor for Easter, and left on Tuesday. At what time did he go?'

'Before my wife and I did. Say half-past nine. We had a party here on Easter Monday and one of the guests lost an earring. After she had gone Adrian found it, and rang to arrange with her to drop it in on Tuesday morning on his way back to Oxford. She was Miss Henrietta Legge of Loxford. Perhaps I should explain that Adrian is my legally adopted son and a couple of years older than

55

Richard. He is a lecturer in Classical Archaeology at Oxford and was due to leave from Heathrow early yesterday to visit some excavations at Ephesus.'

'Thank you, sir. That's all quite clear,' Inspector Bosworth said, putting away his notebook. 'We hope to trouble you as little as possible as we carry on our enquiries, but we are bound to be around a bit, I'm afraid.'

In the meantime intensive police enquiries had been continuing their course. Every adult connected with the farm in the valley was questioned, and one of these, Joe Dadds, a tractor driver, was prepared to swear that he had seen Adrian Morley standing on the edge of the quarry with the old dog from the Manor about 9.40 on Wednesday morning. The most intensive questioning failed to shake him that this had been on Wednesday and not Tuesday morning.

''E must've gorn off whilst I wur turnin' the tractor,' he said. ''E wurn't thur no more when I looked up again.'

Mr Stephen Ash stated that he had seen Mr Adrian Morley drive past Hob's Cottage at about half-past ten on the previous Wednesday.

Three witnesses were located in Buckford who remembered seeing Adrian driving through the village at about 10.30 or a bit later on the Wednesday morning.

This information was conveyed to Inspector Bosworth and he receive it with dismay. The last outcome of the whole unfortunate affair that he would welcome was the possible involvement of a member of a leading gentry family. Most reluctantly he drove to Brading to put the situation before Chief Superintendent Loosemore. Pre-occupied with the entirely unforseen development, he noticed an unusual number of people hurrying along a street, all in the same direction, and on taking a turning leading to the police station he came on a crowd of people being controlled by several constables. He stopped and enquired from one of the latter what was up.

'Woman and three kids done in. Nasty business. That house over there,' the man said, indicating a small terrace house under police guard. 'Neighbours noticed the milk wasn't taken in and rang the station. The chap who lived there's vamoosed.'

Bosworth's heart sank. Chief Superintendent Loosemore was unlikely to listen sympathetically to the Glade Manor problem under the circumstances.

When he was ultimately admitted to the Chief's office he found him decidedly harassed.

'What the hell's up at Buckford?' he was asked. 'Can't you cope with it yourself? The CC will be here any minute now.'

Bosworth stated the situation as concisely as he could. The Super, a fair-minded man, listened with growing attention and finally gave an abrupt nod.

'My God!' he said. 'How we're going to cope with this on top of the business across the road and a major burglary over at Little Longcroft, plus the run-of-the-mill stuff, I just don't know. Here's the CC from the sound of it.'

The Chief Constable of Downshire, was a brisk clear-headed type, adept at quickly summing up situations.

'You've landed a packet all right, Loosemore,' he commented. 'Obviously you people can't tackle it all. The best thing seems to me is for you and your chaps to concentrate on the murders across the road and the armed robbery at Longcroft Castle, and for me to apply to the Yard for somebody to take over this rather odd affair at Glade Manor. Better for an outsider to come along and antagonise the gentry over there. The Morley lot are quite somebody. Then as soon as whoever it is shows up he can take the enquiry on and free you,

57

Bosworth, to lend a hand with one of these other cases. Any comments?'

Both Chief Superintendent Loosemore and Inspector Bosworth expressed emphatic agreement.

'Right,' said the CC. I'll get on to the Yard at once.'

Half an hour later he was called back.

'All fixed up,' he said on replacing the receiver. 'They're sending along that ace bloke, Pollard, if you can believe it. Chance of a lifetime for you, Bosworth. He'll be here with an Inspector Toye about 7. Get suitable accommodation fixed up, of course. Now Loosemore, about the manhunt for the maniac over the road . . .'

Chapter 5

As the Yard Rover headed westward late on Friday afternoon Chief Detective Superintendent Tom Pollard stretched out his long legs, and proceeded to give his colleague, Detective Inspector Gregory Toye, what information he could about the case awaiting them at Brading. A tall loose-limbed man with a deceptively relaxed expression, Pollard presented a complete contrast to Toye. The latter only just made regulation height, and his steady dark eyes surveyed the world through large rims.

'The setting of the murder,' Pollard told him, 'is an estate belonging to the Morleys who have lived at Glade Manor since about 1800. The present head of the family is John Morley, aged 62, who lives there with his second wife, Rose. His son Richard and daughter-in-law Gail occupy the Dower House which is just a few minutes away. There is also an adopted son, Adrian, a lecturer in Classical Archaeology at Oxford who came home for Easter.

'On Easter Monday the family gave its traditional alfresco lunch party, in the course of which a woman guest lost an earring. This was subsequently found by Adrian who made a détour on his way back to Oxford the following day to return it to its owner. He was due to leave for Ephesus on early Thursday in connection with a dig going on there.

'Emily Gover, the murder victim, can fairly be described as having been an integral part of the current Morley set-up. She came to them about 30 years ago, saw Adrian and Richard through the pre-boarding school stage and stayed on as a sort of housekeeper. A little flatlet was made for her, and she was in complete charge when the Morleys were away. As you will have gathered by now the family is pretty warm. Some of the lolly comes from Morley's Book Restoration, a small, very high-class firm which restores disintegrating or damaged antiquarian books. It has been going since about 1900. The works are in the village of Buckford, about three miles away. John Morley is a recognised expert in the field, and Richard is being progressively prepared to take over the business in due course... That about sums up the background, I think. Any point you'd like to raise?'

'No suggestion that Gover had outstayed her welcome, I take it?' Toye asked.

'None whatever, I gathered from the AC. It seems to have been a case of genuine mutual affection which survived the death of the first Mrs Morley and continued under her successor. Right then, I'll summarise what's happened this week. Adrian left about 9.30 on Tuesday morning for Oxford, making a détour to hand over the earring to its owner who lives at Loxford. He was due to fly out to Ephesus early on Thursday to visit some excavations that are being carried out. John, Rose, Richard and Gail left in two cars at approximately 10.30 to attend a wedding at Frinchester, a distance of about 200 miles, travelling more or less in convoy, and lunching en route. Miss Gover — let's call her Nanky for short — remained in charge at the Manor, the daily staff going off for a couple of days' break at the end of the afternoon, to make up for having worked on Easter Monday at the party and cleaned the place up on Tuesday.

'Richard and Gail Morley returned home on Wednesday evening. John and Rose took an extra day off and got back to Glade Manor at about 4.30 p.m. on Thursday afternoon. As they drew up at the front door they were amazed to see the letter box stuffed with a copy of *The Times* and a quantity of mail, and there was no sign of Nanky or the dog. While they were having a hasty look round the house Gail appeared to welcome them back. She said that neither she nor her husband had come up to the Manor since they had arrived back on the previous evening. By now seriously worried, John Morley rang the Works and asked Richard to come home at once. The two men went up through the woods behind the house to the path along the crest of the ridge where Nanky frequently took the dog for a walk. They returned badly shaken, and reported that her body and the dog's could be seen at the bottom of a quarry, and that there were obvious signs of what looked like a struggle at the edge. John Morley then dialled 999. Tell me if you've got the hang of all this before I carry on . . . '

About half a mile later Toye announced that he had got it in focus so far.

'Right. I'll carry on then,' Pollard replied. 'The upshot of the 999 call was the arrival of Inspector Bosworth and support from Brading. He did all the right things, including posting a bloke at the scene of the crime, searching Emily Gover's flat for a possible letter making a date with somebody up on the ridge, and getting by telephone statements of arrival and departure times of the Morley family checked here, and at the wedding, and at the pub where Mr and Mrs Morley senior spent Wednesday night, and with the owner of the earring which Adrian Morley returned to her on Tuesday

61

morning. I'll come back to that in a minute. Everything was going along nicely when Bosworth's men started bringing in statements from people who said they had seen Adrian Morley around on *Wednesday* morning. One was a chap driving a tractor who had noticed him with the Morley dog looking down at the quarry at about half-past nine. Another was a man who owns a cottage on the road just before you get to the Glade Manor drive entrance, and several people claimed to have seen Adrian Morley driving through Buckford, outward bound so to speak, at somewhere about half-past ten or a bit later. Bosworth reported this information to his Super. As the poor chap already had a quadruple murder on his plate and an armed robbery, they decided to push the Glade affair on to the Yard. So here we are.'

'I reckon there's the whale of a lot of checking up to be done,' Toye commented after a lengthy pause. 'What were you going to say about that earring?'

'Doesn't Loxford suggest anything to you, old man?'

In his amazement Toye all but committed the enormity of taking his eyes off the road.

'You can't mean —'

'I can. The earring belonged to Miss Henrietta Legge.'

'Well I'll be jiggered!' Toye exclaimed.

'At any rate there'll be one witness of Adrian Morley's movements on Tuesday morning we can rely on.'

Henrietta Legge had played an important and tragic part in an investigation Pollard and Toye had carried out in Loxford a few years previously.

'I rather think we're reaching the overspill of Brading,' Pollard said as they drove through an increasingly built-up area.

Ten minutes later they found a space in the car park of the police station and presented themselves to a harassed-looking sergeant at the reception desk. There was an atmosphere of urgent preoccupation and of almost continuous coming and going. Chief Superintendent Loosemore received them with unconcealed relief.

'I've never been more thankful to pass on a job,' he said, after summing up the Glade Manor situation. 'We'll give you all the help we possibly can of course. Inspector Bosworth here's been working all day on getting together a case file for you, but it's far from complete, of course, at this early stage. We've booked you in at the White Horse, just five minutes from here.'

'Thanks very much,' Pollard replied. 'What I'd like to suggest is that my colleague and I go over the file to date over a meal at this pub. Then perhaps Inspector Bosworth joins us there in — say a couple of hours — to clear up any points and discuss what strikes us as the best move to start off with tomorrow morning. Of course I realise that you want him back on your other cases as quickly as possible.'

A fleeting expression of surprise and satisfaction passed over the square and rather impassive face of Inspector Bosworth.

'I'd be glad of the opportunity, sir,' he said.

'Right, over to you then, Mr Pollard,' the Chief Super said with evident relief.

The Manager of the White Horse at Brading was gratified by the advertisement value of housing the Yard pair, and offered them a private room with a telephone for a meeting with Inspector Brading after dinner.

When they were settled down with drinks, Pollard raised his glass.

'Cheers,' he said. 'Here's to quick work on a case which looks small-scale and straightforward, but I'm beginning to have a few qualms. Thanks to your spadework, Bosworth, we're at least in a position to consider priorities. What are yours up to date?'

'I take it we ignore motive, sir, and go out for opportunity?'

'Certainly. It looks like being one of the most motiveless killings that I've come across. No luck with the mental hospitals in the area over a homicidal lunatic at large, I take it?'

'None so far, sir. So leaving that possibility my mind's been on opportunity.'

Pollard and Toye both voiced approval and agreement, and produced a rough draft on this aspect of the situation which they had drawn up over their meal. Half an hour later the three men contemplated a joint summary of the five members of the Morley family's activities during the crucial period.

JOHN AND ROSE MORLEY

Could they have killed EG before leaving for the wedding at about 10.30 a.m. on Tuesday? No one else in house. Improbable, because of (i) lack of time if Adrian Morley did not leave Glade Manor until 9.30 a.m. (ii) They could not have removed Wednesday's *Times* from the Glade Manor letter box.

RICHARD AND GAIL MORLEY

The suggestion that they carried out the murder before leaving at 10.30 a.m. on Tuesday is not on if Adrian did not leave before 9.30 a.m. In any case Nanky would have been occupied with breakfast for John and Rose. They could not have returned home from the wedding before about 7.15 p.m. on Wednesday. In theory they could have gone up to Glade Manor and somehow got Nanky to go up to the top of the ridge at some time between their return and Richard's arrival at the works on Thursday morning, removing Wednesday's *Times*. Check up the time their daily woman arrived and left on Thursday and of Richard's arrival at the Works.

ADRIAN MORLEY

Check time of his arrival at Miss Legge's home in Loxford on Tuesday morning. Investigate reports that he was seen in the Glade area on Wednesday morning. Was there any known reason for his coming back so soon? Did he actually leave for Ephesus early on Thursday morning?

STEPHEN ASH

Only near neighbour of Glade Manor and the Dower House. Can he confirm any of the above reports of the comings and goings of the Morleys, or did he see anyone else about? Has he been in residence roughly between 10.30 a.m. on Tuesday and 4.30 p.m. on Thursday? He has only recently bought Hob's Cottage. What is known of his past history?

NB An important point is whether anyone is known to have seen Nanky after Adrian Morley left Glade Manor on Wednesday morning.

'Well,' Pollard said, stretching luxuriously and clasping his hands behind his head 'this analysis gives some idea of the very intensive work you and your chaps have put in between Thursday evening and our turning up tonight. Hats off to all of you, don't you agree, Toye? You've given us a flying start on the job.'

Bosworth expressed rather confusedly what a privilege it had been to co-operate with the Yard. Anything more that the local force could do had only got to be asked for, whatever other jobs were on hand. The session ended warmly over a further round of drinks, and Toye saw him off.

When he reappeared Pollard remarked that it looked like being a hell of day ahead, and that they'd better cash in on what sleep they could get.

'I think the best thing would be to split the essential bits of checking up between us,' he said. 'Adrian Morley's comings and goings are obviously a priority. Because of our previous dealings with the lady I think you'd better be the one to go over to Loxford tomorrow morning, and check up on his visit to Miss Legge on Tuesday morning to return her lost earring. Quite simple for you to slip in a question about Wednesday morning, and look out for any reaction from her. Then come back to Buckford, and with your usual ingenuity check up on Richard Morley's time of turning up at the works on Thursday morning. In the meantime I'll go over to Glade Manor and chat up John Morley and his wife, and then go on to Hob's Cottage and see what sort of a chap this Stephen Ash is, and if he saw any of the alleged comings and goings on Tuesday and Wednesday mornings. Of course he was ideally situated to commit the murder, especially with both the Morley households away, but as he's only just arrived in the neighbourhood he doesn't look like a very likely candidate. We'll meet up at a pub for lunch, pool our findings and plan our next move. Does this all make sense to you?'

Toye, gratified at being entrusted with the interviewing of Henrietta Legge, replied that it looked all right to him. With his usual efficiency he produced an Ordnance Survey map, and they agreed on a village within a few miles of Buckford for their meeting.

'Bound to have a pub of some sort,' Pollard said. 'Let's call it a day, then. I'll just get on to the Yard and ask for an investigation of Stephen Ash's past life.'

Within a few minutes of arriving at Glade Manor on the following morning Pollard privately conceded to himself that it was inconceivable that either John or Rose Morley had murdered Nanky, as he had now come to think of her. It was impossible to believe that the signs of grief

66

apparent in them both were not genuine. But official routine had to be carried through, of course ...

They all three sat in the library, and after apologising for distressing them further he explained that in a murder investigation all statements had to be checked and cross-checked.

'Of course,' John said. 'We fully understand. So go ahead.'

Without hesitation they confirmed their departure on the previous Tuesday morning at approximately half-past ten, roughly an hour later than Adrian's. Nanky had stood on the front door step, waving them off.

'We gave a few toots as we passed the turning to the Dower House,' John went on, 'and waited for about a minute for my son and daughter-in-law to follow on. We travelled more or less in convoy the whole way, stopping for lunch at an hotel. The Cross Keys it was called, wasn't it, Rose?'

'Yes,' she replied. 'At Wrenford. We started off again at two. I remember looking at my watch and thinking that we were making good time so far.'

Pollard thanked her and made a brief note. Petite, with a fair colouring like her husband's she was charming in appearance in spite of the grief and exhaustion in her face, he thought. He went on to check their overnight break of journey on the way home and the time of their arrival at Glade Manor on Thursday afternoon.

'When did you first realise that something was wrong, Mrs Morley?' he asked her.

'Why, the moment we drew up at the front door. The letter box was crammed with mail and a copy of *The Times*. Nanky would never have left it like that all day.'

Pollard went on to extract an account of their anxious search of the house, including Nanky's flatlet, the arrival of Gail to welcome them back and the call to Richard at the works.

'Even then,' John said, ' the thought of an attack on her somewhere in the grounds never entered our heads. We more or less took it for granted that she'd had a stroke or a coronary while taking our old dog for a walk in the woods.'

'Then your son, Mr Richard Morley, arrived, and you went up through the woods to the top of the ridge and saw the signs of a struggle on the edge of the quarry and what had happened?'

'Yes. As soon as we got back to the house I put through a 999 call.'

There was a brief pause. Pollard registered that the library was a beautiful room with some good portraits in the spaces between the bookcases.

'That was John's first wife,' Rose said, indicating the most prominent one, 'and my dearest friend.'

An attractive face, Pollard thought, and full of character. A strong one . . . .

'Perhaps before you see him I ought to explain that Richard is Fenella's son,' John said with a gesture in the direction of the portrait. 'She died from heart failure after a few days' illness ten years ago.'

'Thank you for that information,' Pollard said, 'and both of you for being so patient over my tedious routine questions at this difficult time. I must move on and make a nuisance of myself elsewhere. Do you see much of your nearest neighbour at the cottage on the other side of the river?'

'Not so far,' John replied. 'He only bought the place a few weeks ago and we hardly know him as yet. He seems to have spent a good deal of his life in Australia, and going to race meetings is apparently one of his main interests. We invited him to a party on Easter Monday, but he had fixed up to go to the Bank Holiday meeting at Westingham with a chap he'd met while househunting.'

'There's just one other matter before I go. I know that Inspector Bosworth's men have searched Miss Gover's flat and found nothing to throw any light on her death, but as the case has now been handed over to the Yard, I and Inspector Toye, who is my assistant, must go over it too. It's difficult at this stage of the enquiry to plan ahead, but I hope it won't be very inconvenient if we turn up some time within the next few days?'

'Please come at any time,' John Morley replied. 'Our one wish is to get this ghastly business cleared up. I understand that the inquest will be opened on Monday morning and adjourned for a fortnight after the usual preliminary steps, and we have made arrangements for the funeral to follow on Tuesday.'

On emerging from the gates of Glade Manor Pollard turned left and drove the short distance to Hob's Cottage. He left his car in the road and walked up a short rutted drive badly in need of resurfacing and weeding. The cobbled courtyard in front of the cottage had a derelict appearance with weeds springing up between the stones, and what was apparently the cover of a disused well was overgrown with bindweed. Work on the cottage itself had started. There were heaps of planks, bricks and other building material, and a ladder leading up to the roof was in position. The front door of dark oak studded with nails was half open, and he walked up to it.

'Anyone around?' he called.

There was the sound of feet coming down steep uncarpeted stairs and a man in dirty jeans and an open necked shirt appeared. Pollard placed him in his early sixties. He was short and powerfully built with a deeply sun-tanned face and untidy greying hair. He was also badly in need of a shave.

'Mr Stephen Ash?' Pollard enquired, holding his official card.

The man took it and slightly raised shaggy eyebrows. He made a gesture towards Glade Manor.

'A cop,' he commented. 'You're on the job over there, I guess? There's damn little I can tell you,' he added, in a marked Australian accent.

'Sorry to disturb you when you've got so much on hand, Mr Ash, but I'd be glad if you'd answer a few questions.'

'Anything to oblige. How about sitting on those planks over there? It stinks of damp and dry rot inside.'

'Good idea,' Pollard replied. 'I won't hold you up long.'

They sat down in the sun. Stephen Ash took out a packet of cigarettes and held it out.

'Forgot you were a cop,' he said as Pollard politely declined. 'Not my idea of one,' he went on, lighting up.

'You've taken on a packet here,' Pollard remarked, looking around. 'What brought you to this part of the world? Quite a way from Australia.'

'When I came out of the army in '45,' Stephen Ash replied, expelling a cloud of smoke, 'my one idea was to put as big a distance between myself and the bloody mess of Europe as I could, and Australia looked like filling the bill. I'd no ties back here, so I picked up my gratuity and pushed off. I worked my way up in a building firm in Sydney, and didn't do too badly. Ended up by owning a few bits of property. Then the sort of thing you read in books happened. An advert in a paper. A firm of solicitors at a place I had never heard of called Brinkleigh, up north, were trying to trace me. They'd got some information which would be to my advantage, the advert said. Over the phone I heard a great-aunt I'd forgotten existed had left me thirty thou' in round figures. I was knocked flat. Came home and picked up the dough. Something in the smell of the place seemed to get me. I went back, settled things up and came back for good. Being a builder I decided to buy cheap and recondition a place. Somewhere down south. England's bloody wet and cold after Sydney. This just filled the bill. End of story.'

'I can see it's got possibilities,' Pollard commented, looking across at the cottage. 'Do you see much of the people over at Glade Manor?'

'Blimey, no! We aren't on visiting terms. That set-up's too county and pre-war for the likes of me, even if they haven't a handle to their name. To be fair they've been quite decent to me when we chance to meet. Asked me to some binge or other on Easter Monday, but I'd fixed up with a bloke I'd met when I was house-hunting to go along to Westingham races.'

Pollard took out his notebook.

'What I've come for, Mr Ash, is the checking up of statements which has to be done thoroughly in a murder investigation, I'm afraid. Put your mind back to last Tuesday, will you? Did you notice anyone come out of the Manor drive in a car and go past your gate fairly early in the morning?'

Stephen Ash reflected, scowling and scratching a stubbly chin.

'Yeah,' he said. 'About half-nine. Youngish bloke in a red Austin Maestro, heading for Buckford. He'd been around over Easter. Son of the house, I'd imagine.'

'Did any other people you recognised go that way later on Tuesday morning?'

'Nobody I saw. I was working inside mostly.'

'Did the chap in the Maestro show up again?'

'I didn't see him come back Tuesday, but he went off Buckford way again Wednesday morning.'

'What time?'

'Let me think. I had two lots of stuff delivered that morning by van, and he had to slow down and edge past. That was Carter's van from Brading delivering tiles, about half-ten. Little's, the paint people, came later.'

'Seen the chap since?'

'Nope.'

'Have you called at Glade Manor or the Dower House any time this past week?'

'Christ, no! Didn't I tell you we're not on visiting terms?'

'As you know, Mr Ash,' Pollard continued equably, 'Miss Emily Gover, the Morleys' old nurse, has been murdered by the crude method of pushing her over the edge of a quarry on the far side of the ridge on which Glade Manor stands. Please think very carefully before you answer this question. Have you seen any person, male or female, wandering about this area alone during Tuesday, Wednesday, or Thursday up to 4;30 p.m. this week? Especially during the late morning or afternoon of Wednesday?'

Stephen Ash scratched his head.

'Nope,' he said. 'I'm dead sure I haven't. But I'm doing a job on this joint I've bought, and I don't have my eye on the bloody road all day.'

After extricating himself with the frustrated feeling of having learnt nothing new, Pollard drove to the wayside pub between Loxford and Buckford where he had arranged to meet Toye for a snack. He arrived first, put through a call to Athanasius College, Oxford, and had a conversation with the head porter. He then rang his office at the Yard, and was put through to a department which specialised in investigating the past histories of people who were arousing the interest of the police.

'This bloke Stephen Ash that I rang you about last

72

night,' he said. 'I dropped in on him unexpectedly this morning. He was perfectly willing to talk. Roughly 60, I should say. Emigrated to Sydney after coming out of the army, and worked in the building trade, doing reasonably well and ending up with a bit of money. Then a great aunt left him some cash and he decided to come back to England. He's bought a more or less moribund cottage and is restoring it himself as his retirement home. Unfortunately it's on the doorstep of Glade Manor where the housekeeper was murdered whose demise I'm investigating. It seems very unlikely that Ash is involved but we're virtually clueless at the moment so I'd thought I'd better let you know what I'd unearthed up to date.'

'Thanks,' said the expert. 'It fits in with what we've got on to so far. Nothing much of even possible relevance, I'm afraid. Where can I get you if we do discover anything?'

Pollard gave him the number of Brading police station, and after a brief exchange of friendly badinage they both rang off. Toye had already arrived and they settled down in a corner of the bar with bread and cheese and a remarkably good local ale recommended by the landlord.

'I'll kick off, shall I?' Pollard said. 'Well, apart from the fact that Thursday's *Times* was in Glade Manor letter box when the Morleys got back in the afternoon, I'm dead certain the two senior Morleys are completely out of it where the murder's concerned. Really genuine distress gets across to one. The most useful bit of gen I've picked up this morning came from Stephen Ash at Hob's Cottage. He's a disgruntled sort of chap in spite of having come in for a useful bit of cash from a relative, as he told Bosworth, but didn't show any sign of having it in for the Morleys apart from resenting their superior social set-up. He's registered Adrian Morley and says that he saw him about the place over Easter, and heading in the Buckford direction about half-past nine on Tuesday morning. Ash said he was working inside the cottage and didn't see the two cars of the rest of the family go past later. But he volunteered the statement that he also saw Adrian heading Buckfordwise at about 10.30 on Wednesday. He was more or less sure of the time because a van from a firm called Carter was delivering him some tiles, and Adrian had to edge his car past their van. That's roughly the gen I've collected. I've also rung the Yard and put them on to vetting Ash's past history, and Athanasius about Adrian's early start on Wednesday morning. I got on to the head porter.'

'Well,' Toye said, 'I've been to Morley's Book Restoration and chatted up Richard Morley about his doings from Wednesday evening onwards, and got exactly what Bosworth's given us. On the way out I managed to get talking with one of of the book-binding staff, a very decent sort of chap who said he'd seen Mr Adrain starting off in his car for some outlandish place about half past ten on Wednesday, and wondered if the family had managed to contact him yet. He confirmed that Richard had turned up for work at the usual time — 9 o'clock — on Thursday.'

'Good enough on Adrian's return on Wednesday for some reason, don't you think?' Pollard said. 'It's now been vouched for by Ash and your chap, and the tractor driver who saw him on the ridge, as well as one or two of Bosworth's chaps' witnesses in Buckford. Well, did you get anything out of Miss Legge? Has she changed much since the Railsdon affair?'

'She looks a bit older, as you'd expect, but she's still easy on the eye,' Toye allowed. 'More cash in the kitty, I'd say. The cottage looks as though quite a bit's been done to it.'

'Railsdon had probably settled money on her before we caught up on him, and his daughter who married young Crabbe would have absolutely refused to take it back if I'm any judge of character. Did you get on to the subject of Morley's return to the neighbourhood on Wednesday?'

'I made out that I was a bit confused about Tuesday and Wednesday, and she said without any hesitation that she hadn't seen him again after Tuesday, and that he'd gone out to Ephesus to look at some ruins or whatever. Takes all sorts, doesn't it?'

'Your apparent lack of interest in the place shocks me. What about the Epistle to the Ephesians? As a sidesman at your parish church I should have expected you to enjoy Adrian Morley . . . . Only pulling your leg, old man.'

Toye grinned and asked what the next step was to be.

'John Morley again, I think. He might possibly know some reason for Adrian's movements on Wednesday. With any luck we'll find him at Morley's Book Restoration. Easier to talk to him there than with Mrs M. around, don't you think? I'll settle up here and we'll push off.'

On enquiring at the Works they learnt that Mr Morley had just returned from lunch at home. No, they didn't normally work Saturdays but there was an urgent job on. They were shown into a small room and were told that he would see them shortly. He came in after about ten minutes, still looking shaken and tired, but greeted them both courteously.

'Sit down, Mr Pollard, and there's another chair over there, Inspector. I only hope you've come to tell me that you've made some progress in this ghastly affair. I feel it's put years on to my life.'

'I'm afraid we've nothing much to report up to date, sir,' Pollard replied. 'At this state it's largely a matter of clearing the ground. I understand that Mr Adrian Morley left Glade Manor at about half-past nine on Tuesday morning, about an hour before you and Mrs Morley and your son and daughter-in-law. We know that he left Loxford, where he handed over a missing earring to Miss Legge who had lost it at your party on the previous day.'

'This is all perfectly correct.'

'Were you expecting him to return to Glade on the following day, Wednesday, before leaving for an archeological expedition at Ephesus early on Thursday?'

John Morley looked astonished.

'There was never any suggestion that he intended to. If he did, I can only imagine that he had left something essential behind. Notes on the work he intended to do at Ephesus, for instance.'

'We have two witnesses who are prepared to swear that they saw him here on Wednesday morning. One is a labourer who was driving a tractor on the farm in the valley below the crest of the ridge behind the Manor. This man also swears that the dog was with him. The other witness is Mr Stephen Ash of Hob's Cottage. He saw Mr Adrian driving past at about 10.30 a.m. I have been in touch with the porters' lodge at Athanasius, and there is no doubt that Mr Adrian spent Tuesday night in his rooms there, and arranged for an early call on Wednesday morning, saying he had to come down here to collect some papers before leaving for Ephesus by an early flight on Thursday morning. He did not intend to return to Oxford but to drive straight from here to London and spend Wednesday night there.'

The three men sat without speaking for several moments, Pollard unobtrusively observing the signs of grief and stress in John Morley's face.

'Well, Chief Superintendent,' the latter said at last, 'quite obviously anyone who was physically fit and within range of my house in the middle of this week is a potential suspect. It seems beyond doubt that as a result of his return visit to Glade on Wednesday that my adopted son Adrian falls into this category. As I told you, I have no idea why he came down to Glade again on Wednesday, but his statement to the porter at Athanasius that he had left some important papers behind seems to me a perfectly reasonable one. If Mr Ash saw him driving away in the direction of Buckford at about 10.30 on Wednesday morning, it looks as though he must — since he made an early start from Oxford — have spent roughly a couple of hours at Glade. Assuming that Nanky was still alive when he arrived she would, I am certain, have insisted on giving him a second breakfast. In theory he could have persuaded her to go up to the top of the ridge with him and murdered her there. But I find this second suggestion preposterous, and utterly unacceptable to anyone who knows Adrian. He and Nanky were devoted to each other. She had cared for him from when he was a month old until he went to his preparatory school. Whenever he comes down here he earmarks some time for having elevenses or tea with her, or for taking her out in his car. I may add that I have telegraphed to him at an address that he left with me, and that he'll be returning home as soon as possible.' John Morley paused briefly. 'Of course I understand that you are bound to go into the movements of anyone who could have been responsible for this murder.'

'Thank you for being understanding about my unenviable job,' Pollard said. 'I shall, of course, be obliged to question Mr Richard Morley and his wife about the time of their return to the Dower House on Wednesday evening. An exceedingly helpful piece of information would be evidence of Nanky having been seen by someone after Mr Adrian Morley left the area at about 10.30 that morning. I have been wondering if any tradesmen call regularly at Glade Manor after this hour on Wednesdays?'

John Morley picked up the telephone receiver and began to dial a number, an impassive expression on his face.

'My wife would know,' he said, passing the receiver to Pollard.

Rose Morley took the call.

'Tradesmen or anyone who calls regularly on Wednesday mornings, Mr Pollard? Let me think. The milkman, of course, very early. About 7. Newspapers come about 8.30, and the post soon afterwards. And that's all, I think. Laundry is delivered and collected on Fridays, and the baker's van comes three times a week: Tuesday, Thursday and Saturday. I do the rest of the household shopping in Buckford personally, although I might ring up in an emergency. The shop people are most helpful if that happpens.'

Reflecting that the Morleys were undoubtedly the type of customers likely to get prompt attention in an emergency, Pollard thanked Rose Morley, and passed on the information to her husband. He had hardly finished doing so when the telephone rang. John Morley snatched up the receiver.

'My wife. A call from Adrian,' he told Pollard hurriedly.

Pollard sat waiting, occasionally catching a word, while John Morley occasionally interjected a terse question, and finally rang off.

'Barring accidents, Adrian will be back in London some time tomorrow evening,' he said, a note of unmistakable reassurance in his voice. 'It's a question of getting a flight from Istanbul at such short notice, but apparently people are being most helpful. He's ringing

78

again when he's fixed up. Incidentally the coroner's office rang just now to confirm that the inquest will be at 10 o'clock on Monday morning in the parish room here. Presumably it will not matter if Adrian can't make it on time?'

'Not in the least. It will simply be a matter of a burial certificate being issued and a request by us for an adjournment. Are there any questions you want to raise, Inspector?'

'No thank you, sir,' Toye replied.

'Then we needn't take up any more of your time, Mr Morley, and thank you for your help,' Pollard said, getting to his feet.

When they went back in the Rover Toye gave him an enquiring look.

'All hearsay up to date, isn't it? But all the same, you know, Adrian Morley's Wednesday morning trip does lend itself to a reasonable explanation which it would be difficult to disprove.'

'It makes Richard Morley and his wife a bit more vulnerable, doesn't it?' Toye said thoughtfully.

'Quite. They have no resident help according to Bosworth, and were presumably on their own at the Dower House from about 7 on Wednesday evening until Richard went off to the works next day. Their daily woman doesn't come until half-past nine .... I know,' Pollard went on after a pause, 'that it was hammered into us from the day we joined the force that opportunity was the thing to go for, but there comes a point in an investigation when it makes sense to see if the personality of suspect makes him or her more or less likely to seize the opportunity. I admit that by our time checks Rose and John Morley are out of it, but even if they hadn't been I would have been prepared to count them out on personality grounds.'

'Well, if the young couple are out of it too, I suppose we switch over to Adrian?'

'Your guess of the outcome of that step is as good as mine,' Pollard replied rather gloomily as they drew up outside the Dower House.

Richard Morley appeared at the front door accompanied by a black-and-white cocker spaniel.

'Mr Richard Morley, I think?' Pollard enquired, holding out his official card. 'This is my colleague, Detective Inspector Toye.'

'Good afternoon,' Richard replied formally. 'We have been expecting you. Come in, please.'

He paused as Pollard came in.

'I just want to tell you that my wife is pregnant,' he said. 'Our first. I'm very anxious that she shouldn't be upset in any way.'

'Thank you for telling me, Mr Morley,' Pollard said. 'I'll bear it in mind.'

He followed Richard into a pleasant sitting room where Gail was sitting in an armchair by the window. She looked rather pale, he thought.

'Chief Superintendent Pollard and Inspector Toye,' Richard told her. 'My wife, Superintendent. Sit down, won't you?'

As he spoke he took a chair facing Gail's. Pollard drew up another and Toye installed himself in the background. As he sat down Pollard observed the strong resemblance between Richard and his father and the similar signs of strain in their faces.

'There's a statement my wife and I want to make before you question us,' Richard cut in rather abruptly. 'It is that the mere idea that we murdered Miss Gover — Nanky, we always called her — is so utterly preposterous that it's difficult to react rationally. We were, like my parents, devoted to her. This applies even more to me

80

than to my wife who only came to know her after we were married.'

'Let me just explain the lines we're working on,' Pollard said easily. 'In theory anybody within easy reach of Miss Gover while she was walking the dog at the top of the woods is a potential suspect. With the help of the local force we are carrying on the enquiries into local residents' activities set in motion by Inspector Bosworth. Other neighbouring forces are helping with information about, for example, unstable people in their areas. In short, we're interested in anyone who had the opportunity to commit what appears to be an utterly senseless crime, and are not concerning ourselves with motive at the moment.'

'Thank you,' Gail said. 'I get the idea. My husband and I had first-class opportunity but not the vestige of a motive. Quite the reverse. Ask us anything that might possibly help.'

'Yes, go ahead,' Richard added. 'Sorry if I was abrasive.'

'Just run through everything you can remember about what happened when you got back here on Wesnesday evening.'

Gail leant back in her chair frowning slightly in the effort to recall details blotted out by subsequent developments.

'Our daily had left a hotpot simmering in the oven,' she said, 'and we had a meal almost at once. Say half-past seven. It had been a morning wedding with a jolly good wedding breakfast, but we pushed off as soon as the happy couple left and didn't stop for any tea.'

'Why were you in such a hurry to get home?' Pollard asked.

'Work,' Richard replied. 'We've got a major job on at our book restoration business, and it was important for either my father or myself to get back. As it was, the senior hand that we'd left in charge rang me before we were through with supper.'

'What time would that have been?' Pollard asked.

'Oh, about 8, or a few minutes after, I shoud think.'

'Did you have any other calls that evening?'

'A friend rang me later to fix up a round of golf at the weekend. James Didcot from the village. He's in the phone book. About ten past nine that call was, I think. My wife had gone up to bed.'

Gail thought she caught a look of slight surprise on Pollard's face and smiled.

'We'd better come clean,' she said. 'I've started a baby, Chief Superintendent. At last. Of course I'm being urged on all sides to go easy, and I admit that the wedding trip was a bit wearing, so I went up to bed after we'd had some supper. Say half-past eight.'

'May we offer congratulations and good wishes?' Pollard said. 'Thank you for telling us.'

'I followed on after I'd had a look at *The Times*,' Richard added, 'and taken James Didcot's call. About a quarter to 10. We were dead to the world until the alarm went off at 7.30 on Thursday morning. No proof of any of this, of course, but I can only say that we've given you the facts. I clocked in at the Works at just on 9.'

'And our daily woman arrived as usual at 9.30,' Gail added. 'There's just one other thing that's occurred to me. I didn't go up to the Manor to have a word with Nanky on Thursday morning, what with unpacking and telling our daily all about the wedding, but I gave her a ring before lunch and didn't get an answer.'

'Did this surprise you?' Pollard asked.

'Well, just fractionally. I should have expected her to be getting ahead with a meal for the parents on Thursday night. but I've noticed lately that her hearing isn't quite as good as it used to be, and thought that she was probably out in the vegetable garden. Anyway, I was going up to welcome the parents back in the afternoon.'

'Just one more question. Was your daily woman working here in your absence on Wednesday?'

'She did some spring cleaning for three hours in the morning, and has said she didn't see or hear anything that would link up with Nanky's death. You'll want to check up with her. Her names is Mrs Polts and her address is 10, White Lane, Buckford.

'Thank you,' Pollard said, glancing at Toye who was jotting down the address in his notebook. 'One more thing has just occurred to me. Have either of you had any contact with the new occupier of Hob's Cottage, Mr Stephen Ash?'

'Only to pass the time of day if I happened to run into him in Buckford,' Richard replied. 'This awful disaster of Nanky's death has rather driven us in on ourselves, I'm afraid.'

'I've seen him in the distance once or twice but never spoken to him,' Gail added quietly.

'Thank you,' Pollard said. 'That really is all. Before we go, I wonder if I might use your telephone in case any further information connected with the case has come in? I don't want to bother them at Glade Manor again.'

'Certainly,' Richard replied. 'Come along to my study.'

A few minutes later he learnt from John Morley that Adrian had just rung him to say that he had managed to get a seat on the late afternoon plane from Istanbul to London on the following day. He would come down by car and drive straight from Heathrow to Glade, but might well not arrive much before midnight.

'Well,' Pollard remarked as they drove away from the Dower House, 'the more I see of the Morleys the more

83

certain I am that they hadn't a hand in the murder. But we haven't had a chance of questioning Adrian yet, so my opinion isn't conclusive. That Wednesday morning trip of his down here puts him into a rather different category. Somehow or other it sticks in my throat a bit. He doesn't sound at all the type of chap to leave important papers behind when he's just going to take off for an archaeological trip to a place like Ephesus. Did he leave them behind to provide himself with a pretext for a return visit to Glade before going abroad, and if so what was his motive, for heaven's sake? Look here, Toye, going off at a tangent I want to go up to the ridge behind Glade Manor to look at the exact spot where Nanky and the dog were sent over the edge. You go on into Buckford, and interview the Richard Morley's daily woman. Then wait for me on the road before it gets to Hob's Cottage, out of Ash's sight, and I'll join you there.'

Pollard left the Glade Manor drive at its junction with the road and cut up the ridge on his left through the trees. On arriving at the crest he followed it for a short distance to the right. All traces of the murder had been meticulously photographed by Inspector Bosworth's men, and the prints awaited him in his room at Brading, but photographs in his opinion were incapable of conveying that elusive thing, atmosphere. He began by inspecting the trampled undergrowth behind a clump of shrubs. That was where the chap waited for her to come along, he thought. Snapped off stems and twigs in the low hedge along the edge of the quarry showed where Nanky had put up a pathetically useless struggle against her assailant. That would be the thorn bush where a fragment of her cardigan had caught, now carefully preserved with the photographs at Brading police station. He studied traces of the footprints in a damp patch of soil where the actual struggle had taken place. There were obvious male prints, partly obliterated by overnight rain, traces of a small serviceable woman's shoe and poignant traces of the dog's desperate attempt at resistance, his claw marks cutting across the other prints.

Walking a short distance further on Pollard got an open view of Glade Farm in the valley at the foot of the ridge. Parts of the farm house looked old and interesting, but there were also modern functional buildings, and the land around looked in good heart. A recently ploughed field opposite the point where he was standing would, Pollard thought, be where the tractor driver had glanced up and seen Adrian Morley on the Wednesday morning. In terms of distance the recognition of someone you were familiar with would have been perfectly possible, he decided.

He made his way slowly through the woods down to the road to rejoin Toye, feeling very dissatisfied with his progress on the case up to date. To begin with it seemed that, in default of further evidence, one had got to accept that the two Morley couples were out of it. Timing . . . the word seemed to echo in his mind with an odd persistence. Then quite suddenly it linked itself with Adrian. Why, if he had to make that early start from Oxford on Wednesday, did he hang about for at least two hours at Glade, if Stephen Ash's statement at seeing him driving towards Buckford at about 10.30 was reliable? What did he want with all that time and an expensive night in London before getting an early morning plane to Istanbul on Thursday? A girl-friend? Then why the delay in starting off from Glade? Pollard's mind moved on rapidly to Adrian's proposed return journey, leaving Istanbul by a late afternoon plane and probably not turning up at Glade until about midnight on Sunday?

85

Istanbul time would be about three hours ahead of London time, so if he left at 5.00 p.m. by their time and the flight took about three hours he would arrive at Heathrow at about 1700 GMT. Obviously the thing to do was to find out by telephone calls what other planes would be available for him tomorrow. It might all be quite irrelevant, but there seemed something odd about his comings and goings . . .

Anyway, Pollard thought, rounding the corner beyond Hob's Cottage and raising a hand in greeting to Toye seated in the Rover, it gave one the illusion of doing something. Toye looked at him enquiringly as he got into the passenger seat.

'Back to Glade Manor?' he asked.

'No,' Pollard replied. 'I've got a hunch that the most paying line for us at the moment is to concentrate on Adrian Morley. Back to Brading for a bout of telephoning.'

Chapter 6

A small room with a telephone had been allocated to Pollard and Toye at Brading police station. As soon as they reached it Pollard picked up the receiver and asked for a priority call to be put through to his office at Scotland Yard.

'What luck,' he said within a couple of minutes on hearing his personal assistant's voice. 'I didn't think you'd be on seeing it's Saturday afternoon. Look here, I want some urgent calls put through right now. The top priority is one to the airport at Istanbul. I want the departure times of all planes leaving for London tomorrow, and the time they're due here. OK? Right. The second call's to get a car registration. I only hope they haven't closed down for the weekend. I want the registration number of a red Austin Maestro belonging to Adrian Morley of Athanasius College, Oxford. When you've got the number, find out if the car's parked at Heathrow. It'll be in a medium- or long-stay car park. If you can't get the registration number try the car park people, and make it sound terrifically urgent. There can't be all that many red Austin Maestros in any particular type of car park, and anyway there must be tickets with retained counterfoils when people put their cars in. Morley would have parked his on Wednesday afternoon or evening, or very early on Thursday morning of this week. When you've got these enquiries in the bag, ring me back here — Brading police station. Toye and I will fill in time brooding over the unilluminating file. Sorry to unload all this on you on a Saturday afternoon, James ... Right? Cheers.'

Toye had already extracted the file from his brief-case and placed it on the table. On ringing off Pollard clasped his hands behind his head and stretched out his long legs under the table while contemplating the file with distaste. The telephone rang suddenly, quite unexpectedly.

'Good Lord, surely James can't have got any info already,' he said, snatching up the receiver. 'Yes, put him through, will you?' he replied to the Brading operator. 'Oh, hallo,' he said, and, turning to Toye, mouthed "Hayford, from investigations." Have you any more of interest following enquiries about this Stephen Ash down here?'

'Nothing much, I'm afraid, beyond what you got yourself from Brading. Home background, war service and post-war emigration all verifiable. Also the cash left by a great aunt, a Mrs Clara Firth, and Ash's settlement of his affairs in Sydney and final return to the UK last January. Subsequent house-hunting in the southern counties and the arrival at a cottage near Buckford. There's only one thing that might possibly interest you. He worked his way up in Australia into small-scale property dealing after what must have been a pretty tough spell in the building trade, and at one stage had an unofficial partner called George Rendell. They were both run in for shady dealing, but Ash was discharged after preliminary questioning. Rendell went to trial, was found guilty and given a couple of years. He got maximum remission and came out last summer. The two men didn't join up again, and apparently there was some

88

feeling that Ash had contrived to shift the blame for the dirty work on to Rendell.'

'Thanks a lot,' Pollard said. 'Beyond the fact that Ash's cottage is the nearest inhabited building to the house where our murdered housekeeper was employed and to the married son's place, there's no reason to suppose that he was in any way involved in her death, especially as he's arrived here so recently. It's one of those virtually clueless cases, worst luck. Anyway, thanks for getting the checking-up done so quickly.'

He put down the receiver.

'Well, that's that,' he said, 'presumably leaving us with Adrian Morley as sole suspect at the moment.'

'There's the makings of a case against him,' Toye observed. 'Coming down to Glade again on Wednesday morning as he did. Fetching papers could have been a trumped-up excuse. You wouldn't expect anyone of his standing to start off on an important journey bound up with his job to leave important papers behind, would you?'

'No,' Pollard said thoughtfully. 'You wouldn't. And if he wasn't getting a plane to Ephesus until Thursday morning, why come back to Glade so early on Wednesday? He'd have known that the daily women were having a couple of days off and that Nanky would be alone in the house all day. And why attract attention to himself by driving through Buckford at a busy time of day when he was almost bound to be noticed? And where was he going? Not back to Oxford. I asked the head porter at Athanasius when I rang. Where the hell *did* Morley go?'

'To ground, at Heathrow?' Toye suggested.

'Possibly. But I don't think it's worth contacting all the hotels within a reasonable radius at this stage, though, until we see if he turns up tomorrow. When we get the arrival times of bloody incoming planes from Istanbul we'll mount a watch at whichever car park he's left his Maestro.'

'Obviously,' Pollard said during a lengthy pause in which he executed a complicated doodle on a spare sheet of paper, 'Adrian Morley had opportunity, created by himself. So perhaps it's legitimate for us to consider motive at this stage. What imaginable motive could he, a man of his type and position, have had for brutally murdering an elderly woman he'd known all his life? And he was and always had been devoted to her, according to John and Rose Morley. And it wasn't a case of a sudden mental blackout, seeing the careful planning behind the job.'

'Something she'd found out about him and threatened to tell the Morleys?' Toye propounded unconvincingly.

'I think it's important to remember that Adrian Morley's a highly intelligent bloke,' Pollard went on, as if he had not heard Toye's remark, finishing his doodle and crumpling up the piece of paper. 'Frankly I simply can't believe that if he'd wanted Nanky out of the way for some unimaginable reason he'd have done the job in such a incompetent fashion.'

As he pushed the case file away from him with a gesture of rejection the telephone rang once again, and he snatched up the receiver and listened.

'Put me through,' he said on being asked if he would accept a call from his office at New Scotland Yard.

A couple of minutes later he knew the registration number of Adrian Morley's car, and in which long-stay car park it had been left at Heathrow. He also learnt that contact had been made with the airport at Istanbul, and that the times of flights to London on the following day would be available shortly.

'Damn good work by all concerned,' he told James Halliday. 'We'll wait.'

As they waited Pollard propounded a course of action for the following day. Continuous cover of the exit from the car park would be essential. They themselves in the Rover would take over shortly before the arrival time of the first probable plane.

'We'll have the exit covered overnight,' he said, 'but I'm all but certain that he won't materialise until tomorrow. One's got to try to look into the chap's mind of course — if he's the sort of bloke everyone seems to think he is — he'll be badly hit by Nanky's death and want to get back to Glade. On the other hand he's a scholar of some standing, and will want as long at Ephesus as he can decently take. My guess is that he'll turn up later rather than earlier, but he may, of course, have another long and at present unexplained interval between landing at Heathrow and arriving at Glade very late. Take my point?'

Toye replied that he did, while expressing doubts about the ability of other Yard drivers to trail the Austin Maestro successfully.

'Harper might be OK,' he said dubiously. 'Or perhaps that young Pomeroy or —'

A further telephone call interrupted his speculations. Pollard listened intently, jotted down a list of departure and arrival times and ended with heartfelt appreciation of James Halliday's efficiency.

With Toye he studied the list carefully. After some discussion they agreed that to be on the safe side they would take over car park observation for an incoming jet due at 1130 GMT.

'The next one's due at 1400 GMT,' Pollard said. 'We can take it in turns to go and get some lunch. We'd better ring our long-suffering homes and tell them to expect us tonight when they see us. And I'll ring the Yard, of course. We can get back from here in three hours, barring accidents, and I want a really top driver laid on to be briefed about tomorrow morning. If Morley's car goes out he's got to tail it come hell and high water. I think that's the lot for the moment, except for a word with Bosworth if he's around.'

Inspector Bosworth, involved up to the hilt in the local crime wave, looked exhausted, but listened to Pollard's resumé of ground covered up-to-date in the Glade Manor case with interest.

'Blimey,' he reacted. 'All I can say is that if this chap Adrian Morley did the old nurse in he must be clean off his nut. It only seems a possibility because there just isn't a sniff of another lead up to now, is there? The chap we've left on to deal with any reports coming in has just told me there hasn't been a single one. Not even a hoax try-on. Well, Super, good hunting and we'll keep at it down here. Get on to the Yard in a split second if anything turns up.'

'We know we can rely on that all right,' Pollard said. 'I only wish it would.'

They made good going in spite of the Saturday night traffic and arrived at the Yard a few minutes before 10. On reaching his office Pollard asked the inevitable question, only to be told, as he expected, that no information connected with the Glade Manor case had come in.

'Only the usual half-dozen loony phone calls and letters, sir,' the sergeant on duty told him.

'Is Constable Harper here?'

'Yes, sir.'

'Send him in, will you?' Pollard said, making for his own room, followed by Toye.

He had used Detective Constable Harper as a driver on several previous occasions and had been impressed with his personality and driving expertise. These impressions were confirmed as the young man knocked, entered and stood smartly to attention.

'You may sit,' Pollard told him. 'I've got an important job lined up for you in connection with a case of murder which Inspector Toye and I are working on at the moment. It is possible, but by no means certain, that a suspected murderer may arrive by plane from Istanbul at 8 o'clock tomorrow morning. You will report to the official on duty at the gate of the long-stay car park for the use of travellers on inter-continental flights.'

As he talked he was aware of Constable Harper's riveted attention.

'That's all, I think,' he said finally. 'Recap, will you?'

The recap was faultless. Toye, invited to comment, raised a point so trifling that Pollard suspected a flicker of amusement as Harper respectfully disposed of it.

'Right then,' he said. 'We'll consider it settled. Be on duty by 8.00 a.m. tomorrow morning, presenting your credentials to the official in charge who will be expecting you. If the car we've been discussing comes out, you tail it relentlessly but as unobtrusively as possible. The Heathrow people will notify the Yard if it doesn't. Inspector Toye and I will relieve you at approximately 10.45 a.m. in readiness for an Istanbul plane due in at 11 o'clock. Contact my office here by phone if and as required. Any questions?'

'None, thank you, sir.'

'You'd better go and get some sleep, then.'

'Sir.'

Detective Constable Harper rose, stood erect, saluted and withdrew.

The grandfather clock in the hall struck two as Pollard let himself into his home in Wimbledon, the chimes dying away into a deep silence. The scent of lilac hung in the air, and on switching on his torch, he saw a great jar of white and purple sprays on the chest by the sitting room door. He crept noiselessly upstairs and gently pushed open his bedroom door which Jane, his wife, always left ajar when she knew that he was going to be very late. She stirred a little, and he went over to the bed, stooped down and kissed her.

'I'm back, darling. Go to sleep again. To — sleep — again.'

The familiar formula worked. Jane Pollard relaxed and sank back into oblivion. Within a few minutes of slipping into bed beside her he drowsed into sleep himself, having left a note about his programme for the morning on the dressing table.

He woke to broad daylight and the sound of people trying to be quiet just outside the door, and grinned to himself. After a short interval, someone opened the door cautiously, and his son Andrew's head came tentatively round it. Pollard produced a gargantuan snore which evoked a burst of laughter as both Andrew and his twin sister Rose precipitated themselves into the room and on to the bed. Simultaneously Jane appeared in the doorway.

'It's just struck 8,' she announced. 'Breakfast at 8.30. Come off it, brats, and let your father get up.'

She shooed the twins out of the room, went across to the bed and took the hands Pollard held out to her.

'All right? Doubtful? Or a blank wall?' she asked.

'Doubtful, certainly. Blank wall a definite possibility.'

'I seem to remember having heard this before,' she told him. 'Followed by a recantation.'

However critical the stage of his current case Pollard always found his family's mealtime babble a restorative. On this occasion Andrew, already determined on a career in agriculture, was being fetched for a day on his uncle's

94

farm in Sussex. There was a possibility that he might even be allowed to drive the new tractor. Jane and Rose, who had inherited her mother's artistic gifts and was considered promising, were going up to London to visit an exhibition of Japanese art at the Tate.

'We're taking a picnic lunch to eat in the park,' Rose retorted to a taunt from her brother about wasting a super day indoors. 'Daddy, will you be mostly indoors or out?'

'Quite a bit on the road, I think.'

'In the Rover, Dad?' Andrew asked. 'It's a great car,' he declared on getting an affirmative answer, and launched into an enumeration of its merits.

Jane and Rose exchanged pitying glances. Pollard leant back in his chair and surveyed the red gold of his family's hair, faithfully inherited from their mother by the twins. A quarter of an hour later the trio waved him off from the garden gate. Feeling much refreshed he turned into the main road and let his mind switch over to what the next step could possibly be if Adrian Morley turned out to be a dead end. Toye and the Rover, both impeccable in appearance, were awaiting him at the Yard. So, too, was a message from Istanbul airport. No passenger of the name of Adrian Morley had boarded the jet due at Heathrow at 1100 GMT.

On the way down, Toye broke a lengthy silence with the inevitable question.

'Say this chap Adrian Morley's got a watertight explanation of what all his comings and goings have been in aid of,' he said as they cruised westward at a decorous 70 mph. 'Where do we go from there?'

'Just what I'm chewing over, old man,' Pollard replied. 'Unless an unexpected new candidate pops up the only option I can see is going back to Stephen Ash whom we've written off.'

The Yard's advance programme at Terminal Three had gone smoothly into action. An interested car park manager guided Toye to the appropriate gate.

'Not all that much doing at long stay this morning,' he said. 'That young chap you've posted here's got his head screwed on all right. Sits at the wheel not looking particularly interested, but I'll wager he knows every darned car that's come in or gone out.'

The Yard car drew up near the entrance gate, watched without apparent interest by Detective Constable Harper sitting at ease at the wheel of a police car. He started up his engine and vacated the ideal observation and getaway position he had chosen, and Toye moved into it. Harper drew up at a short distance away, locked his car and came over to the Rover, giving Pollard a salute.

'Sorry you haven't had the fun of a cross-country chase,' Pollard said, 'but you've done an essential job. Inspector Toye and I are taking over now, so push off and get some grub. Report to my office when you get back.'

'Sir.' Harper saluted smartly and returned to the police car.

They watched a medium-sized jet smoothly coming in to land and disappear behind buildings.

'Morley could be travelling under an assumed name,' Toye said.

'Doubtful. It takes time to fix that sort of thing up, and he would only have had a couple of days.'

A typical businessman complete with brief-case appeared, showed the car park attendant what appeared to be a ticket, went in, and subsequently reappeared at the wheel of a Renault and drove off. Time passed. Planes took off and landed. Two cars were brought in for long-term parking and three collected by their owners. None of these was a red Austin Maestro. Pollard and Toye, both short of sleep, took naps in turn, Toye being wakened by the arrival of a messenger with a sealed envelope for Pollard who ripped it open.

'No answer, thanks,' he told the bearer. 'This is it, my old and bold,' he told Toye when they were alone. 'The Istanbul airport people confirm that a Mr Adrian Morley boarded the plane for Heathrow at 1400 hours local time today. Get out, and ask the chap on duty at the entrance to show you the Morley Maestro. We'll watch it coming up to the exit and be dead on the beam to follow on.'

After the tedious hours of inaction both Pollard and Toye were aware of mounting tension as 2 o'clock drew on. They watched planes taking off and preparing to land, specks which progressively lost height, gained substance and developed form running clumsily along the ground.

'Roughly medium height and dark hair,' Pollard repeated, with a sudden qualm at the general character of the description. But after what appeared to have become eternity the figure of the man stepping purposefully towards the entrance to the car park suddenly seemed to incarnate the brief description. There was a short pause as he took out a pocket book and presented the gate-keeper with a document. They exchanged a few words, and Adrian Morley — for neither Pollard nor Toye now had any doubts — vanished into the regimented lines of parked cars.

'It's a longish way down on the left,' Toye said. 'I was certain I'd spotted it when I went and had a look over the gate just now.'

He turned the key in the Rover's ignition and began to run the engine gently.

After a few minutes had elapsed there was a sign of movement in the more distant serried ranks of parked cars. Finally, a slowly moving patch of red made its way

97

up the central open track of the car park. Reaching the gateway it came to a halt. A dark head leant out of the driver's window and there was another brief conversation with the man on duty. Something changed hands and the gate was opened. The red car moved past the Rover and bore left as Toye let in the clutch.

Unlike Toye, Adrian Morley was a reasonably competent but not a first-class driver. Clearly anxious to make good going he was frequently edged out of the fast lane as they headed westward. Forced to follow suit, critical mutters came from Toye at intervals.

'Easy,' Pollard said. 'As long as we don't lose him it doesn't matter when we get there. Wherever there is. What price Glade Manor? Pause for laugh.'

'Doesn't do the car any good changing up and down every other minute,' Toye grumbled, falling behind an estate car loaded to the roof.

It was a perfect spring afternoon, and Pollard allowed himself brief spells of enjoyment at the newly shaken-out leaves of trees and occasional patches of primroses. But the niggling anxiety about the next step if the present course of action led nowhere kept recurring to his mind. Better to get the moment of frustration over if that was what they were heading for, he thought, glancing at his watch. As often happened, Toye's mind was similarly engaged.

'Five minutes to the major roundabout,' he said.

As they came up to it the red Austin began to bear left in the company of a smaller but still appreciable stream of traffic.

'Let's face it,' Pollard commented, 'It's beginning to look damn like homeward bound.'

His mind was now preoccupied with possible alternative courses of action related to Stephen Ash ... contact with the Sydney police ... searching Nanky's flat. The local chaps might conceivably have overlooked something in the way of a pointer to her murderer ...

Suddenly an advance notice indicated a turn-off ahead to Shirborough. The right hand indicator of Adrian Morley's Maestro flicked up, and the Rover's promptly followed suit. In a matter of seconds both cars had left the main stream of traffic, and the Rover was immediately behind the Austin. Toye reduced speed.

'It'll look fishy if we don't overtake,' he said, 'so what?'

'Let him go round the next corner and pull in to the side,' Pollard said, grabbing an Ordnance Survey map from the glove compartment.

They pored over it, and he exclaimed aloud.

'Good God! See this turning to Loxford, about six miles ahead? Loxford! That business about an earring the day Morley's supposed to have started off ... Don't tell me that he suddenly fell for Henrietta Legge at the party and all these comings and goings add up to a love affair? If the AC gets on to this I'll never hear the end of it. Here, get cracking and just keep the Maestro in sight. Let the bloke coming up behind overtake us.'

Toye drove with care and skill, keeping just out of sight of the Maestro and stoically enduring the astonished stares from drivers of overtaking cars. Finally they reached the outskirts of Loxford.

A succession of well-remembered buildings brought back the case which had ended in the suicide of the guilty party, wealthy Basil Railsdon of Loxford House. They passed the church and the vicarage, slowing down as the Maestro ahead of them reduced its speed and finally indicated an imminent right turn.

'Pass the turning and pull in close to the hedge,' Pollard said.

Toye switched off the engine, and the two men sat

looking at each other. Pollard suddenly began to laugh. He got out of the car, prospected cautiously up the lane and reported that Adrian Morley's car was parked outside Henrietta Legge's cottage. He glanced at his watch.

'Just after half-past five,' he said. 'Adrian Morley told his father over the blower from Ephesus that he mightn't get to the Manor before midnight, presumably allowing himself plenty of time for making a formal proposal, judging by my personal experience. Let's give them until 6, shall we, while we try to think up our next line of action? Right up your romantic street, isn't it? Don't forget we've still got a case on our hands.'

Toye replied that the whole business would make a top-class film.

They sat talking quietly, ears half-consciously alert to any sound of a car engine starting up at the top of the lane. They agreed that one practical step had to be tackled: the search of Nanky's flatlet in the chance that something relevant to her death might have been missed by Bosworth's men.

'We'll muscle in on that job first thing tomorrow,' Pollard said. 'The only other line that might possibly pay off is delving into Stephen Ash's past. I suppose it's just possible there's some gen from the Yard waiting for us at Brading.' He looked at his watch again.

'Just on 6,' he said. 'Let's go. As usual, I haven't a clue about how best to tackle this rather dicey situation.'

They walked up the lane between hedges frothing with April greenness and the white and gold of spring wild flowers. A blackbird suddenly released a torrent of song. Pollard noted that the little wicket gate had been freshly painted and there was a general air of quiet prosperity. He led the way to the cottage door and rapped gently with its knocker. There was a silence followed by faint sounds of disturbance. Then light footsteps approached the door from within. It was opened and he was face to face with Henrietta Legge after the lapse of more than two years.

He had an excellent memory and the intervening period since they had last met telescoped in a flash. Her indefinable air of breeding, deep blue eyes and distinctive features indicated in some subtle way tension endured, but at this moment overlaid with an unexpected wonder undistorted by his sudden appearance.

'Good evening, Miss Legge,' he said pleasantly, and, he hoped, reassuringly. 'My apologies for disturbing you on a Sunday evening, but we noticed Mr Morley's car outside your gate and are anxious to have a word with him, if we may.' He introduced himself and Toye.

'Good evening.' A youngish man with dark hair and eyes and a highly intelligent but unwelcoming face appeared at Henrietta Legge's side. 'I suggest that we go and sit in my car rather than intrude on Miss Legge.' His tone conveyed annoyance but no sign of apprehension. 'I suppose you've followed me down from Heathrow,' he added.

'Surely it would be much more comfortable if Superintendent Pollard and Inspector Toye came in and you had a chat in the sitting room,' Henrietta said. 'I'll leave you to it while I wash up the tea things and do a few odd jobs.'

Following her to an open doorway on the left Pollard reflected with amusement that this was going to be an equal partnership. The trauma of the Basil Railsdon affair seemed to have toughened rather than shattered her. Assisted by Toye she manoeuvred the tea trolley out of the room and shut the door.

Adrian Morley indicated a couple of armchairs and sat down himself in a third, folding his arms and contemplating his visitors.

101

'To start with it would be helpful, Mr Morley, if you would tell us how much you know about the late Miss Gover's death,' Pollard said, conscious of Toye unobtrusively taking out his notebook.

'Only what my father told me over the line to Ephesus. That when they returned home on Thursday afternoon she was nowhere to be found, and he and my brother Richard discovered her body lying at the bottom of the quarry on the far side of the ridge behind the house.'

'So you, I gather, were the last member of the family to see her alive, on the Wednesday morning?'

'Correct. The others were away at a wedding. Richard and his wife returned on Wednesday evening, but didn't go up to the Manor.'

'All these facts have been checked, Mr Morley. It's your movements on Wednesday that seem to us to call for some explanation. The head porter at Athanasius has stated that you asked for an early call on Wednesday as you had to go home again to collect some papers you had left behind, and that you would be going straight on to Heathrow and not returning to the College. Do you confirm this?'

'I do. I made good time driving down and arrived to find Miss Gover hadn't got the breakfast ready that she was insisting on providing, so I took the dog up to the top of the ridge to stretch my legs. Then-'

'One moment. Did you see anyone on the way up or down?'

'I saw a chap driving a tractor in one of the fields in the valley below the crest. No one else.'

'You then returned to the Manor?'

'I did. Nanky — Miss Gover — had a colossal breakfast laid on for me. I just about managed to get outside it, and went off at half-past ten.'

102

'You drove through Buckford, and out on the the London road?'

'I did.'

'And drove to Heathrow?'

'Yes.'

'Rather early, as your plane didn't leave until 8.30 on Thursday morning. Perhaps you made a diversion en route, Mr Morley? Do you know,' Pollard went on, 'I rather think you came here, didn't you?'

There was a pause. Then, without warning, Adrian rose to his feet. Toye, reacting by making a slight movement towards the door, was checked by a glance from Pollard. Adrian reached it in a couple of strides and opened it.

'Henrietta,' he called. 'Join us, will you?'

He waited to close the door behind her while Toye left his chair and moved to another in the background. As she sat down and looked enquiringly at Adrian, Pollard saw the hitherto resolutely uncompromising expression on Adrian's face suddenly relax into one of amused resignation.

'The Chief Superintendent's rumbled it, darling,' he told her. 'We must come clean. About ten minutes ago,' he told Pollard, 'Miss Legge agreed to marry me.'

'It's unorthodox, I admit,' Pollard said, 'but even if I am conducting a police enquiry, I want to offer my congratulations and good wishes. I'm sure Inspector Toye would like to join with me,' he added, giving his colleague a meaning glance. Toye hastily averted his eyes from Henrietta and concurred.

'It's not quite as sudden as you might think,' Adrian said. 'We've known each other slightly most of our lives, both coming from this part of the world. Then it suddenly came to life at an Easter Monday party at the Manor, didn't it, darling?'

'You know my history over the past few years, Mr Pollard. I shall always remember how kind you were to me at ... at the time. Amanda, Basil's daughter, and Jeremy Crabbe — the vicar's son — have been, too. They have made the cottage across the lane their holiday home, and have been wonderful to me.'

'And now there's the Oxford link,' Adrian said.

'Jeremy and I are both on the strength at Athanasius. But we mustn't waste your time. Can I tell you anything that might possibly help over this ghastly business at Glade Manor?'

'I gather that you found Miss Legge's missing earring and returned to Oxford last Tuesday, making a diversion here to return it to her?'

'Yes. We'd become very close at my stepmother's Easter Monday party, where she lost it, and finding it seemed to provide the ideal opportunity to pop the question, in common parlance. I arrived all geared up, only to find the exuberant Jeremy Crabbe and Amanda on the doorstep, both clamouring for information about how and where I found the thing. There seemed no possible way of getting Henrietta to myself, so while we all sat and nattered I worked out another scheme.'

'I know,' Pollard interposed. 'The important papers left behind at Glade Manor.'

Adrian grinned.

'I wondered if you'd get on to that. I got back to Oxford, rang Nanky — Miss Gover — and fixed to go down early the next day, pick up something that looked like papers and come on here nicely in time to be invited to lunch. I arrived to find the house shut up and the garage open and empty. I waited until 1 o'clock, scribbled a few lines and put them through the letter box, and drove to Heathrow. I won't enlarge on the tedium of the endless evening. I didn't feel like looking anyone up, and it seemed quite hopeless to concentrate on the work I was hoping to do at Ephesus. I went off on the 8.30 plane the next morning.'

'I have to bear in mind that I'm conducting a police enquiry,' Pollard said. 'Can you produce any independent evidence of being in your car outside this cottage round midday last Wednesday?'

'An old boy was cutting the grass at the Crabbes' cottage just opposite and broke off to come over and tell me that Miss Legge had gone somewhere in her car about half an hour before I arrived. He went off himself at about half-past twelve.'

'I heard all about it when I met him in the village the next day,' Henrietta put in. 'I think, incidentally, I ought to come clean myself at this point.'

'The note you found in your letter box when you got home?' Pollard queried with a smile.

'I know I ought to have told Inspector Toye about it when he came to see me on Friday,' she admitted. 'By that time I knew about Nanky, of course, and I just felt I didn't want to involve any of the family in more dealings with the police than was absolutely necessary.'

Pollard consulted his notebook.

'Mr Morley, you could have got a seat on a plane by pleading an emergency some time yesterday, surely?'

'Yes, I could,' Adrian admitted without hesitation. 'But as I was at Ephesus it seemed sensible to do the photography I needed for my new book and wait for a flight today. I knew my brother Richard was on the spot at Glade to support the parents. I gave a later time of arrival there because — well, I'm sure you'll understand — I wanted to call in on Miss Legge on the way home.'

'Our one difficulty where you are concerned, Mr Morley,' Pollard said, meeting Adrian's eyes squarely, 'is that so far we've not been able to find anyone who saw

Miss Gover alive after you left Glade on Wednesday morning. You were seen heading for Buckford by Mr Ash at roughly half-past ten, and also by other witnesses as you drove through the town shortly afterwards.'

'I take your point only too well,' Adrian replied, 'but obviously I'm in no position to produce a witness myself.'

'You are quite certain that as you left Glade you didn't pass a tradesman's van coming up the drive, or one of the endless people who keep delivering unwanted pamphlets?'

'Unfortunately, no. I'm dead certain I didn't.'

Pollard saw Henrietta's grasp of Adrian's hand tighten.

'Well, truth will out, you know. We'll leave it at that for the moment. I take it that you'll be returning to Oxford after the funeral?'

'Yes. I'm not sure which day. It rather depends on if the parents want me to stay for a bit. I'll notify you when I go.'

'Right. Well, we'll be going. We're staying at the White Horse at Brading if anything occurs to you.'

'I'll see you out,' Adrian said. 'Back in a minute, darling.'

He stood politely at the gate as Toye turned the car in the Crabbes' gateway, and raised his hand as it moved off down the lane. Pollard reciprocated. Returning to the cottage Adrian took Henrietta into his arms.

'I've had a great thought, love,' he said. 'You're coming back to Glade with me. A first-rate distraction for the parents, and I'm just not leaving you here to brood over the situation. Go and put a few things together.'

All her life Henrietta was to remember her sudden irruption into the Morley family circle.

106

'They'll be in the library if I know anything,' Adrian said, driving very quietly up to the front door. He helped Henrietta out of the car, linked her arm in his and led her into the house.

'Here we are,' he announced, opening the library door. 'I've brought my future wife along.'

There was a moment of stupified silence before Rose sprang to her feet to embrace Henrietta.

'Darling,' she said. 'It's like the sun suddenly coming out.'

Nothing in the way of fresh information was waiting for Pollard and Toye at Brading police station, and they drove on to the White Horse.

'Mercifully we're not too late for dinner,' Pollard said. 'I can neither think nor talk until I've got some food inside me.'

They worked their way systematically through a solid four-course meal almost in silence.

'Coffee in the lounge, sir?' asked their waiter.

'Yes, please. Lots of it, and very hot and strong.'

'Certainly, sir.'

The lounge of the White Horse was old-fashioned but the chairs were comfortable. After several cups of coffee Pollard stretched, looked across at Toye and grinned.

'I feel quite human again,' he said. 'We'd better consider our priorities for tomorrow. Two, don't you think? One, try to clear Adrian Morley finally and completely by finding somebody who'll state on oath that they saw Nanky alive after he'd left the Glade area by way of Buckford. And secondly, find out if there was somebody who had a link with her that we haven't discovered yet. It may turn out to be a sheer waste of time, but let's search her room ourselves tomorrow. Go through it with a fine comb, so to speak. Bosworth, with his much better knowledge of the area is much better placed to track down anyone who may possibly have seen her on Wednesday after Adrian's departure. I'm beginning to feel there must be a perfectly respectable local who up to now has concealed homicidal tendencies.'

They sat in silence for nearly a minute.

'Of course,' Toye said at last, 'that chap Stephen Ash was perfectly placed for the job. The two lots of Morleys away at the wedding and no other house within sight. Trouble is there's no imaginable link between him and deceased, who's been living at the Manor for the past thirty years while he's been in Australia. He could be your homicidal maniac, I suppose.'

'No suggestion whatever of that in the reports we've had from Sydney. There's always got to be a first time, I suppose, but you can't haul people off to be examined by a psychiatrist just because there seems to be nobody else to fill the bill ... Here, I'm just going to ring Jane to restore my sanity, and then turn in.'

Chapter 7

The preliminary inquest on Emily Gover was typically concise and brief, and Pollard's request for a fortnight's adjournment immediately granted. The coroner issued a burial certificate, and in a quarter of an hour the police were clearing a passage for his car through the crowd hopefully assembled outside. Questioned by reporters, John and Richard Morley who represented the family gave a short account of Nanky's long and devoted service at Glade Manor, and also their opinion that a homicidal maniac must have come into the district, and had been wandering in the woods at the time when Miss Gover was taking the dog for a walk.

Pollard and Toye mixed unobtrusively with the crowd when the coroner had gone, to pick up any remarks on people in the neighbourhood or solitary strangers seen about on the previous Wednesday, but heard nothing of interest. By arrangement with John Morley they eventually returned to their car, drove to Glade Manor and were taken up to Nanky's flatlet.

'Just forget all about us, Mr Morley,' Pollard said after politely declining an offer of elevenses. 'We may be here for some time, breaking off for lunch and going along to the station at Brading in case any information's come through from the Yard.'

He took the key to the door of the flatlet from an inner pocket and slipped it into the lock.

The flatlet consisted of a fair-sized bed-sitting room with a south window. A door opposite the one through which they had come in led to a small well-equipped kitchen and a little bathroom beyond it. Pollard and Toye returned to the main room and stood for a few moments looking about them.

'My guess is that the family provided the fittings and probably quite a bit of the furniture,' Pollard said, 'but left the choice of colour scheme and whatever to her. Good no-nonsense reds and blues seem to have been her taste ... The most likely and helpful find would be a diary or a letter. Suppose you begin with the kitchen and bathroom while I make a start in here. Let's open the window and get rid of the fug, anyway.'

Toye disappeared in the direction of the kitchen, and Pollard took off his coat, hung it over a chair and began a systematic search of the hanging cupboard and its contents. Mercifully, he thought, inspecting a modest number of garments hung on a rail, she wasn't the clothes-conscious type, poor old dear. He took out the hangers one by one, checking every pocket and feeling hems. The garments were all of good quality, if outmoded, and impeccably neat and clean. Nanky had kept her shoes in a tidy row at the bottom of the cupboard and he paid special attention to these but found nothing of any interest secreted in them. He was just replacing the last pair when Toye emerged from the back regions.

'Nothing stashed away out there,' he reported. 'I've had the whole of the stuff in the airing cupboard out, and tipped out every blessed tin. A couple of empty suitcases and a few cardboard boxes with nothing in 'em.'

Pollard sat back on his heels and reported a similar lack of success. He glanced at his watch.

110

'Half-past twelve. I suggest we knock off. Go over to Brading and look in at the station in case there have been any calls from the Yard, and then go and have some grub. Come back and finish this room this afternoon. The books will take a bit of time.' He gestured towards a small but well-filled bookcase. 'A book's an obvious place for hiding a letter if there's one involved.'

They left Glade Manor without encountering any of the family, and drove through Buckford to Brading. A message was waiting for Pollard asking him to call the Yard and get on to the department which had been delving into Stephen Ash's past history.

'Nothing much,' he was told, 'but we thought we might as well let you have it. Sydney rang us to say that they've been unable to contact George Rendell, Ash's former partner, who was found guilty of fraud over some building which the two men were putting up in partnership, you remember, while Ash got off. The bloke seems to have left Sydney for the time being. He's paid three months rent in advance for his flat and left a substantial deposit in his bank.'

'Well, thanks a lot for letting us know,' Pollard said. 'It doesn't seem to tie up with anything at the moment, but we're so stuck that any bit of info's grist to the mill. We're in process of going through deceased's flat with a toothcomb, but no luck so far.'

'Keep going. Darkest hour before the dawn and whatever,' the official said. 'Let us know if you're coming up here or pushing off somewhere new.'

Pollard passed on the gist of the conversation to Toye. It was a still, overcast day, and they ate their lunch in a rather depressed silence while looking through local newspapers. The Glade Manor Murder featured prominently, but nothing dredged up by their reporters threw the faintest ray of fresh light on the circumstances

111

of Nanky's death. References to Adrian Morley were so far confined to his frustrated trip to Ephesus.

On their return to Glade Manor John Morley came out of his study to tell them that the funeral was being held at Buckford parish church at 11 a.m. on Wednesday.

'I expect a lot of people will turn up,' he said. I don't know what the usual procedure is, but would you like a couple of seats reserved for yourself and Inspector Toye, Chief Superintendent?'

Pollard thanked him and asked for a seat for himself.

'Inspector Toye will be among the crowd outside,' he said. 'I believe I told you before that it's surprising what one can overhear on these occasions when locals are milling about.'

Returning to Nanky's flat they resumed their search with grim determination. Toye stripped the bed and investigated the mattress while Pollard went through the drawers of the table and their contents with particular thoroughness. He found no letters or any other evidence of contacts with the outside world.

'The world to her seems to have been simply the Morleys and Glade Manor,' he remarked to Toye.

Finally they turned their attention to the bookcase. Besides a bible and a prayer book there was a well-worn copy of *The Pilgrim's Progress*, and a few religious books for children, some of which Pollard dimly remembered from his grandmother's home when he himself was a child. There were also boys' books of a much later period, perhaps favourites of Adrian and Richard which Nanky had read aloud to them, and a few old-fashioned simple novels.

They replaced the last book, satisfied that nothing in the way of a letter was included in the contents of the bookcase. The final inspection involved taking down the pictures on the walls. The most striking of these was a head and shoulders photograph of Fenella Morley signed by herself which occupied a central position over the mantelpiece. Pollard studied it with interest. Like the portrait in the library it showed a combination of attractiveness and strength of character. He dismantled it carefully, but there was nothing relevant to the case concealed in the frame. There were numerous photographs of Adrian and Richard at various stages of their lives, from the building of sand castles on summer holidays to their graduations at Oxford.

'So what?' Pollard said wearily, stretching himself. 'Nothing left but the bloody carpet and lino. What wouldn't I give for a cuppa. Come on. If she took a bit up to hide something underneath it would be round the edge, of course. You start on the kitchen door side and I'll begin at the window end.'

A few minutes later he experienced a sensation like an electric shock, but bit his lip and managed to remain silent. Immediately under the window the nails keeping down the edge of the carpet had been hammered into place, but inexpertly. Half a dozen of them were slightly crooked, and had not been driven home with the expertise of those on either side. A moment later he was running his hands over the carpet immediately behind the imperfectly driven-in nails, and found that he could feel something flat and thin, its presence undetectable to anyone merely looking down at the carpet from above. He tried to repress a surge of excitement.

'Just bring over that gadget we've got for hoicking up nails,' he said casually.

Years of working with Pollard had attuned Toye's ear to the slightest inflexion in his voice. Within thirty seconds he was kneeling beside him with the tool in question.

'Feel it?' Pollard asked, running his hand over the

carpet. 'Something under here all right. Probably only a bit of strong cardboard to cover a hole in a floorboard. Get up these nails, will you? You're better with your hands than I am.'

In tense silence Toye prised up the nails.

'Go along to the corner and down the side a bit so that we can turn the carpet back.'

Toye removed the nails quickly and efficiently. Finally, and with great care, Pollard folded back the corner of the carpet. Sitting on their haunches they contemplated a packet measuring roughly eight inches by six. It appeared to be a folded sheet of newsprint in a cellophane envelope secured by a strip of gummed paper.

'Gloves,' Pollard said.

Toye was back beside him with a pair of rubber gloves in less than a minute. Pollard put them on and gingerly lifted the packet by its edges on to the small table in the window. They both bent over it.

'Newsprint,' Toye said. 'Yellow and badly faded, but the lab chaps'll be able to do something, wouldn't you think?'

'There's precious little they can't do, given something tangible to work on,' Pollard agreed. 'We'll take it up right away ... Do you see the edge of a photograph where the fold comes? Here, we mustn't let ourselves think we're home and dry. What's the safest way of packing it up?'

They found a cardboard box and remembered a quantity of tissue paper in a drawer.

'If we run into John Morley on the way out,' Pollard said, 'we'll tell him we can't go after all to the funeral. Bosworth can stand in for us. Come on.'

They went out, carefully locking up the flat behind them.

The following day dragged interminably for Pollard while the contents of the packet were being investigated at one of the Yard's forensic laboratories. It had been made abundantly clear to him that the space he took up was preferable to his company, and he reluctantly retreated to his own office and tried to concentrate on matters arising from other cases. At long last he received a summons from the scientist directing the investigation.

'Well, Pollard, we're through your damn finicky job at last,' he was told. 'The bloody newspaper was split in several places. There were two quite different types of folds. One lot dated back a good many years and that's where the splits were. The others were quite recent, and reduced the overall size of the folded paper to make it fit into the cellophane envelope which is quite new. The paper is a sheet of a local rag called the *Clatworthy Evening News*. We've made enquiries and it closed down in 1958. We've also worked on the fingerprints. Those on the recent folds and the envelope are recent, and easily identifiable with those of a Miss Emily Gover, a copy of whose prints you gave us. The others are so faint that in our opinion they're useless for identification purposes. I imagine it's the photograph you're particularly interested in, and we've done some enlargments. The woman's come up particularly well, but the man's not so clear. Have a look.'

He handed Pollard a greatly enlarged copy of the newspaper photograph headed 'Army Wedding'. Underneath it was the statement 'Lance-Corporal Fenella Plume ATS weds Bombardier Stephen Ash.'

Pollard stared at the photograph for so long that Toye moved at his side. The laboratory superintendent laughed.

'Disconcerting discovery?' he asked.

'Shattering, if illuminating,' Pollard replied. 'And it's

115

got to be broken to a third party. By me, presumably.'

'Bigamy?'

'Undoubtedly, from the look for things. The gutter press will go to town on it, of course. However, we can't thank you people enough for all the work you've put in.'

When they were back in Pollard's office Toye asked if they were returning to Brading at once or staying in London overnight.

Pollard reflected.

'Go down tonight, I think. This business has got to be broken to John Morley, and we now work on establishing the contact between Nanky and Stephen Ash. When and where did it take place? Another thing to find out is how Nanky suddenly got hold of this piece of newspaper. My God, I hope there isn't a third party involved. The situation's snarled up enough as it is. You might ring the White Horse at Brading and book rooms again for us for tonight. Say we'll turn up for dinner. Then in the meantime I'll put in hand a top urgent enquiry at St Catherine's House. Were Ash and Fenella Plume ever divorced?'

Some hours later on arriving at Brading police station they ran into Inspector Bosworth.

'Nothing's come in for you, I'm afraid,' he told them.

'All the same, we may be on to something,' Pollard replied. 'Care to hear about it? Come round to the White Horse when we've had some grub. Say about 9.'

Later, on hearing about the search of Nanky's flat, the discovery of the hidden sheet of old newspaper and the outcome of the visit to the Yard, Bosworth was generous in his congratulations.

'Next best thing to our boys having spotted that lump in the carpet,' he declared. 'Blimey, I don't envy you the job of breaking all this to Mr Morley, always assuming there wasn't a divorce before Ash went to Australia.

How exactly do you see the tie-up with the murder?'

'From what I've heard of Emily Gover, alias Nanky,' Pollard said, 'she was a forthright woman of strong character and utterly devoted to the Morleys. But because of the restricted life she'd led in their employment she was inevitably inexperienced about humanity in general. My guess is that she took the utterly foolhardy step of tackling Ash herself. Told him that she'd discovered who he was, and that it stood out a mile that he'd bought Hob's Cottage as the ideal base for blackmailing John Morley about his bigamous marriage to Fenella Plume. She would have told him to clear out lock, stock and barrel, or she'd go to John Morley herself with the evidence she'd got about his — Ash's — identity. The story would have had to come out, but she'd be seeing that he couldn't cash in on it and make John Morley's life a hell of continuing uncertainty. And Ash himself would be a marked man for the rest of his life as far as the police were concerned.'

'What do you think Ash's immediate reaction was?' Bosworth asked.

'I think he'd probably admit that she'd got him by the short hairs and pretend to agree to put Hob's Cottage on the market and quit. At the same time he'd see the obvious advantage of eliminating Nanky. I'm inclined to think that Nanky didn't go over to Hob's Cottage and tackle him until Wednesday morning, having been held up by the telephone call from Adrian at Oxford on Tuesday to say that he was coming back early on Wednesday to collect some papers. We know Adrian left Glade about 10.30 on Wednesday morning *en route* for Loxford to — as he hoped — see Henrietta Legge. Ash would have assumed that the Morleys were likely to return from the wedding they'd been to latish on Wednesday. It was essential to act promptly after Nanky had

117

tackled him. I imagine that he'd been at pains to acquire knowledge about the Morley household's way of life in connection with his projected blackmail, and that an afternoon walk in the woods for Tim, the old retriever, was a pretty regular feature. It would be a gamble worth taking, he would have decided. It might be some time before both branches of the Morley family would be away from home at the same time, leaving Nanky in sole charge. Worth trying, anyway. He's obviously a clever devil, and it came off.'

'I call that a damn good reconstruction, Mr Pollard, if I may say so,' Inspector Bosworth commented. 'Fits like a glove.'

'Thanks,' Pollard replied. 'All that's lacking is proof, unfortunately. The road past Hob's Cottage and Glade Manor's a minor one, and if you remember, Mrs Morley went through the list of tradesmen who call regularly at Glade Manor, and Wednesday was apparently the one blank day in the week ... The next fence is tackling poor old John Morley, and that's got to wait until the records of divorces just before and soon after the end of the war come through. But I think it's possible that we can all but clear Adrian Morley. I'm going to ring him now at Glade Manor and ask him the name of the hotel he stayed in at Heathrow that Wednesday night before he took off for Ephesus. Then ring the hotel and check his time of arrival there. If it fits reasonably with his having left Loxford about 1 p.m. he's a stage nearer being completely in the clear.'

John Morley answered the telephone.

'Superintendent Pollard speaking, Mr Morley. We found it necessary to return to the Yard on Monday evening in connection with the case, and have only just returned. Could I have a word with Mr Adrian Morley?'

'Certainly,' John replied, with the faintest tinge of uneasiness in his voice. 'I'll get him for you.'

'Adrian Morley here, Superintendent,' Pollard was informed after a brief interval.

'Good evening, Mr Morley. Sorry to bother you at this rather late hour, but I think you can probably clear up a couple of points for me. What was the name of the hotel where you spent the night before leaving for Ephesus last week?'

'The Pegasus. Not all that central, but they run their own taxi service.'

'Thanks. The other thing I want to ask is the time you arrived at this hotel?'

'Just on a quarter to five. I remember because I had been hoping that they'd still be serving teas. I hadn't had any lunch.'

'Thanks very much, Mr Morley. Good night.'

Pollard rang off and returned to Toye and Inspector Bosworth.

'If the Pegasus confirms what he's just said, he's all but out of it,' he told them. 'If only we could find somebody who saw Nanky alive after he left, though . . . I'd better leave it until tomorrow morning, I think. There'll probably only be a night porter on at this hour.'

A call put through to the Pegasus the next morning clinched the matter. Pollard was informed that Mr Adrian Morley must have arrived before 5 p.m. on the previous Wednesday. Reference to his account showed that he had been charged for afternoon tea, and it was not served after five o'clock.

'Well, that's another useful bit of information,' Pollard told Toye. 'Let's bring the file up to date and brood over it a bit while we're waiting for a call about a possible Plume-Ash divorce.'

Intensive study of the file failed to produce any fresh ideas and the morning dragged. Finally, shortly before 12, a call came through from the Yard. Members of the staff of St Catherine's House had been most co-operative and had helped in the search of divorces in the second half of 1945 and the first half of 1946. There was no record of the marriage between Stephen Ash and Fenella Plume having been dissolved.

Pollard groaned. 'Well, that's that,' he told Toye. 'I've got to go through the whole blasted business with poor old John Morley. Ring the Works for me, will you?'

'His secretary's putting the call through,' Toye said a couple of minutes later, handing him the receiver and evacuating the telephone kiosk.

'John Morley speaking, Superintendent,' came the now well-known rather elderly voice.

'Good morning, sir,' Pollard replied. 'I'm ringing to tell you that an important matter has come to light which I urgently need to discuss with you. Can you give me an appointment for the afternoon? I think the best plan would be for me to come to the works if you're agreeable.'

He heard John Morley almost imperceptibly catch his breath.

'Of course, Superintendent. If it is going to take us a step nearer clearing up this appalling affair I'm only too thankful to meet you anywhere you wish at any hour.'

'Thank you. I suggest, then, that I come to the works at half-past two, if you can manage that hour.'

'As you heard,' he said, turning to Toye. 'Two-thirty at the works. Can't say I like the prospect of this interview. I'd better take along the cellophane packet, I suppose, and the Yard's enlargement of the photograph.'

'I'll parcel 'em up for you,' Toye said, conveying wordless sympathy. 'It's gone 1. Better have a snack, don't you think?'

They settled for sandwiches and coffee. Toye introduced the topic of what the next step would be after seeing John Morley.

'God only knows,' Pollard answered. 'I only hope that a lead of some sort will suggest itself by my seeing him. You'd better drive me over to Buckford and wait in the car. I suppose something might possibly crop up that we'd want to do afterwards.'

Punctually at 2.25 the Yard Rover drew up in the car park of Morley's Book Restoration.

'Thanks old man,' Pollard said as he got out. 'Be seeing you.'

The receptionist was obviously expecting him, and he was at once escorted to the lift and up to John Morley's private office. A few seconds later he was being shown in. Pollard registered a different type of room from the one in which he had previously had an interview with John Morley. With a swift glance he took in a large photograph of what must have been the founder of the firm early in the century: a dignified bearded type. There were some good pictures and a Georgian kneehole desk and chairs, well filled bookcases and a handsome grandfather clock.

John Morley was sitting at his desk. He got up as Pollard came in and pushed the papers on his blotter aside.

'Come in, Superintendent,' he said as the door closed. 'I've given orders that we're not to be disturbed.'

He still looked tired and drawn Pollard thought, but perhaps a little less tense. On Adrian's account possibly?

'Thanks, Mr Morley,' he said, drawing up a chair and putting his brief case on the floor beside him. 'To come straight to the point, Inspector Toye and I have covered quite a bit of ground since our last talk. You remember, of course, that on Monday of this week he and I came to Glade Manor to search Miss Gover's flat. It had already been searched by Inspector Bosworth's men, but because of the apparent total lack of motive for Miss Gover's murder I decided to search it myself with Inspector Toye's help. It's an inappropriate metaphor, but I feel I can say that we left no stone unturned. For instance, every garment was examined and pockets turned out, and every book flicked through. You see, the clue we hoped to find was a letter. But I went through her desk myself and was struck by the complete absence of any personal correspondence. Finally we turned our attention to the carpet and the linoleum surround, concentrating on the outer edges to see if there was any sign of their having been taken up for something to be slipped underneath. To cut a long story short, I found something under the carpet by the sitting room window. My attention was attracted by the fact that just here the carpet tacks had obviously been taken up and not very skilfully replaced. We took up more tacks, folded the carpet back and found this.'

Picking up his brief-case he took out a folder and extracted the original cellophane envelope and a much enlarged copy of the newspaper photograph it had contained. As he did so he glanced up and was struck by an expression of rigid control rather than apprehension on John Morley's face.

'This envelope,' he went on, 'contained a folded sheet of newspaper, yellow with age and its newsprint faded. It was possible to see part of a photograph through the cellophane. Needless to say we didn't attempt to investigate further but took the envelope straight up to one of the forensic laboratories at the Yard. Here the experts succeeded, by chemical and other means, in making the photograph relatively clear and most of the newsprint legible. Fortunately there was a comple single page of the newspaper itself. It turned out to be part of a local evening paper of 14 July 1944 which closed down in the 1950s. From our point of view the vital matter was the photograph and the inscription at the foot of it ... Mr Morley, I deeply regret having to do this but I must ask you to look at it.'

As he handed over the enlarged photograph he saw that there was no longer apprehension in John Morley. It had been replaced by an expression of great sadness. The hand holding the photograph shook slightly.

'Don't be distressed on my account, Superintendent,' he said quietly at last. 'You see, I know that Fenella and I were never legally married. She told me herself shortly before she died.'

There were some moments of intense silence in the room.

'But,' John Morley went on, 'she did not tell me the name of her lawful husband ... That bloody scoundrel Ash ... daring to land himself here on our doorstep.'

'Obviously with blackmail in mind,' Pollard went on. 'At the moment we have no proof that Stephen Ash murdered Miss Gover. But assuming that he knew that she had somehow discovered his former relationship with the late Mrs Fenella Morley, he certainly had a strong motive to silence her. A point I want to clear up as soon as possible,' he went on after a pause, 'is how long had she known that your marriage to Fenella Plume was invalid?'

John Morley leant back in his chair and closed his eyes for several seconds, looking, Pollard thought, pathetically old and tired.

'I simply can't believe,' he said, opening them again, 'that she can have known for more than a very short time. She was so devoted to Fenella and Richard, and, I may say, to myself, that the shock of suddenly finding out the true facts of the situation would have been beyond her powers to conceal from us. Looking back, I can say that in the run-up to Easter she hadn't been showing any signs of tension or distress that I noticed, or that other members of the family remarked on. She certainly looked a bit tired after Easter, but the house had been fuller than usual, and my wife's Easter Monday party always involves quite a bit of work for all of us.'

'This suggests,' Pollard said, 'that she had only very recently discovered the facts about Fenella Plume and yourself at the time of her murder, and the hiding of the sheet of newspaper points to the fact that it was where she got the information. How do you think that it suddenly came into her possession?'

John Morley sat up abruptly.

'God!' he exclaimed. 'It's only just occured to me, Nanky had a step-sister considerably older than herself. They had seen very little of each other after Nanky grew up, and about ten years ago the step-sister was allotted an almshouse in the Midlands. Nanky went up to the funeral. I drove her to the station at Brading myself. Richard went into Brading to meet her and brought her back to the Manor, and I distinctly remember seeing him carrying two suitcases through the kitchen towards her flat, so she brought an extra one back. I can also re- member — and my wife would bear me out — Nanky saying she wasn't going to bother about the stuff she'd kept from her sister's almshouse until after Easter and the party were out of the way, and Rose and I were away for a couple of days at a wedding. Don't you think that this suggests that the newspaper photograph of Fenella and Stephen Ash was among the things she'd brought back? It could easily have been with a few calendars or pictures which Nanky had bundled into the suitcase.'

Pollard stared at him, suddenly struck by a flash of illumination.

'It's just occurred to me,' he said, 'that the step-sister may not have "kept" that sheet of newsprint in the sense of deliberately holding on to it, but by sheer chance used it to line the suitcase. I've seen my wife lining one of hers with tissue paper if she was packing some rather special things. This idea would explain the different kinds of creases in the newspaper which the lab people at the Yard commented on. Fitting a sheet of it into the angles of the case would have caused the splits, too, in poor quality post-war paper. Do you know if the step-sister lived at Clatworthy before moving into an almshouse?'

In reply John Morley pressed a switch on his desk to contact the Works secretary.

'Get me Mr Richard, will you, Miss Adams?' he said.

'Hullo, Dad,' Richard's voice came over the line a few seconds later.

'Superintendent Pollard's here, and there's something he wants to know where you might be able to help. Or failing you, we'll try Adrian. Where did Nanky's old half-sister live before she went into her almshouse?'

'Wait a moment while I dredge it up from nursery days ... Cadbury ... Calthrop ... I've got it! Clatworthy, in Midshire. For some obscure reason Adrian and I thought it was a funny name, and used to go about shouting Catsworthy and Batsworthy and so on. Nanky went to see her there once, I remember.'

'Thanks,' John Morley said. 'Actually you've provided a useful bit of information.'

He sat looking at Pollard with frank admiration.

'Where do we go from here?' he asked.

'In my experience,' Pollard said, 'short of a sudden mental breakdown, it is unusual for an average man with a clear record as far as serious violence is concerned suddenly to commit a brutal uprovoked murder. At the moment there isn't enough evidence to warrant charging

Ash. I propose to contact the Sydney police again about him. Meanwhile, as this will take a little time, I think it will be worthwhile to get in touch with the firm of Northshire solicitors who advertised in Australia newspapers in the hope of contacting him. They would probably have been in touch with the police about his identity. I shall go back to London tonight and get an interview with my Assistant Commissioner tomorrow morning about the next step in the case.'

He looked up to see a worried expression on John Morley's face.

'To be frank,' the latter said, 'I'm anything but happy about the situation here at the moment. There doesn't seem to be any doubt that Ash is a dangerous, violent man. Both the Manor and the Dower House are isolated, and the road's a minor one carrying very little traffic, especially at night. If Ash got the slightest inkling that there is evidence against him over Nanky's murder I feel that there might be further violence. My wife and I are not young, and Gail, Richard's wife, is pregnant.

'I do realise all this,' Pollard replied, 'and I've been considering the best steps to take for your protection. To begin with I shall ask Superintendent Loosemore at Brading to provide cover for tonight. I'm sure you can fix up suitable arrangements for the chap on duty. The Brading murderer has been run to earth, so there shouldn't be any great difficulty in providing manpower out here for a day or two. I shall suggest that a 24 hour traffic census is set up on the grounds that the road is dangerously narrow and needs widening and straightening. There will be a sentry-box type of shelter for the chap on duty who will record all traffic going through, and it will be placed at a point where the entries to your two houses and Hob's Cottage are visible, and also the stepping stones over the river. Do these measures reassure you?'

'Completely,' John Morley said. 'I'm more grateful than I can say. Forgive me, but I have had absolutely no idea up to now that the police were so imaginative.'

'We have to be if we're to keep ahead of the criminal fraternity. I'd also like to suggest that if you come across Stephen Ash you keep up the normal friendliness you have been showing him up to date. And I'm sure you'll keep what I have told you this afternoon under your hat.'

'You can rely on that, I assure you.'

Chapter 8

At 10.30 on the following morning Pollard presented himself at his Assistant Commissioner's office.

'Come along in, Pollard, and take a pew,' the latter said, pushing aside the papers in front of him. 'I was beginning to wonder if I was going to be taken into your confidence over this case of yours. Cigarette? No, you never do now, do you? Well, fire ahead.'

'There's been precious little to report to you, sir, until yesterday,' Pollard told him. 'Almost as a last resort Inspector Toye and I more or less took deceased's flat at Glade Manor to pieces and spotted a slight bulge under the carpet. We yanked it up and found a cellophane envelope with the sheet of a now defunct evening paper inside. It was badly creased and split in several places, but the lab boys here made a super job of it yesterday, and at last we had a breakthrough. Miss Gover possessed knowledge which made her a serious potential threat to Stephen Ash. I suggest that he had looked forward to a steady income from blackmailing Morley by his arrival on the doorstep of Glade Manor.'

'She must have been an utter fool to tackle Ash single handed and expect to manage to head him off the Morleys for good,' the AC commented.

'Inexperienced in the ways of the world rather than a

fool I think, sir,' Pollard replied. 'She'd had precious little experience of the seamy side of life.'

'What was the blackmail for?'

'Could be that Stephen Ash was married to John Morley's first wife — Fenella Plume — and there was no divorce.' The Assistant Commissioners whistled. 'But.' continued Pollard, 'we've no actual proof that Ash murdered Miss Gover. Only that he had ample opportunity to chuck her over the edge of the quarry between the time Adrian Morley left the Manor at about 10.30 on the Wednesday morning, and Mr and Mrs Richard Morley's return to the Dower House at roughly 7 o'clock that evening. And as well as opportunity he had a very strong motive to silence her for good. There was no other way in which he could blackmail John Morley in safety.'

'How do you suppose Ash got on to Fenella Plume's marriage to John Morley?'

'That's one of the matters I think it would be worth discussing with the solicitor who dealt with Stephen Ash's great aunt's Will and estate. We can ask him if there were any letters handed over to him among her possessions after her death, and if so, did he pass them on to Ash. It's possible that one of the old lady's pals wrote to her and said what a splendid match dear Fenella Plume had made to a wealthy man down south near Brading. Old ladies rather tend to keep letters. Imagine Ash's reactions if he chanced on information of this sort. Extraordinary coincidences do happen, but it really does seem a bit much to swallow that he should have landed up in a cottage a few hundred yards from the Morleys by pure chance. It suggests to me that he made enquiries and realised that he was in a position to blackmail a wealthy man who'd pay up to protect Fenella's reputation and conceal the fact that their son Richard was illegitimate.'

The AC leant back in his chair and contemplated the ceiling for a few moments.

'So what you're saying, Pollard, is that you want to track down the solicitor who managed to locate Ash after the great aunt's death and try to find out what was handed over to him as well as cash. Especially if there were any letters. Going to take the hell of a time, isn't it?'

'I don't think so, sir. While I interviewed Ash when I took over the case he happened to mention that the solicitor who located him lived in a place called Brinkleigh, in Northshire. It's quite a small town — the inestimable Inspector Toye has been doing some tracking and I don't think there'd be much difficulty in finding the solicitor, who must have made pretty searching enquiries about Ash from the Sydney police before accepting his *bona fides*. Something interesting about his past might come out.'

'You've got a point there,' the AC conceded. 'All right. Go as soon as you can, and for God's sake hurry up and get back. We're short of chaps with your experience, and this case can't be allowed to drag on indefinitely.'

'Thank you, sir. We'll step on it.'

'We? Toye too, I suppose,' the AC grumbled.

'You agree, sir, I take it, that Adrian Morley can be let off the hook on the strength of the Gover-Ash link we've now unearthed? The only remaining ground of suspicion against him is that we haven't yet found anybody who admits to having seen Gover after Morley left for Loxford about 10.30 on the Wednesday morning.'

'Cross the chap off the list,' the AC replied, 'and go all out for Ash.'

Pollard returned to his office and summoned Toye who received the news of the drive to Brinkleigh and back with satisfaction.

130

'Thought it would come to that,' he observed. 'When do we start?'

'After a very early lunch. Say 12. I've one or two things to settle first.'

His priority was contacting Adrian and he was duly put through to Glade Manor. Rose Morley answered the telephone.

'Oh, good morning, Superintendent. I'm afraid my husband's over at the Works.'

'Actually it's Mr Adrian Morley I want to speak to,' he told her. 'Is he around?'

'He's in the garden, I think. Just hold on and I'll get him for you.'

Pollard thanked her and waited, drumming gently with his fingers on his desk while a programme for Brinkleigh took shape in his mind.

'Adrian Morley here,' he heard.

'Mr Morley, I'm ringing to tell you that we're no longer interested in you as far as this case is concerned,' he said.

'Very decent of you to let me know officially, Superintendent. I can't honestly say I've been worrying about being run in on suspicion, but it's good to know that I'm officially cleared. I suppose there's no need for me to stay around? I really ought to get back to Athanasius some time tomorrow at latest.'

'No. None whatever. If we should want any information from you, we'll ring Oxford.'

'Thanks. An impromptu engagement party tonight, I think. You would have been a welcome guest.'

'I appreciate that,' Pollard said. 'All good wishes to you and Miss Legge for your future happiness.'

He rang off, reflecting that there were occasional rewarding moments in a detective's life.

Adrian strode out into the garden where he and

131

Henrietta had been doing some weeding. He sensed a tenseness in her as she looked up at his approach.

'Shades of the prison house are apparently not going to close about your future husband, darling,' he told her. 'Pollard has just rung to say he's no further interest in me.'

As he took Henrietta into his arms he realised that she was trembling, and guided her to a garden seat.

'After a slightly melodramatic start,' he went on, 'we now get down to the severely practical. When and where are we going to be married? House-hunting in Oxford and whatever. Not to mention the summer term and schools. The hell of a lot to do, in short. Look, there's Rose, hovering. She's astute, you know, and probably sensed from Pollard's tone that I was in the clear.'

'All's well,' Adrian told her. 'I've been struck off Pollard's list of suspects.'

Rose Morley embraced them both with rapturous exclamations.

'A party.' she exclaimed. 'Not a proper engagement party — there isn't time. Just ourselves. You'll help me, won't you, Henrietta darling? I know there'll be an unfillable gap, but we've just got to think of how darling Nanky would have loved it. I think we'd better inspect the deep freeze, and Adrian can run over to Brading if we're badly stuck. But you'd better look in at the Works. Adrian, and tell your father and Richard about that nice Superintendent Pollard's call just now.'

Adrian winked at Henrietta.

'OK Mum. Just check up the food reserves and let me know what's wanted.'

Henrietta went with Rose to the larder . . . I belong to these people for good, she told herself half incredulously, and to Adrian totally. She sensed the ebbing away of past tragedies and disappointments and the dread of increasing loneliness in the years ahead.

At the Works John and Richard Morley expressed their satisfaction at Pollard's telephone call with equal satisfaction though in fewer words.

'It was only a matter of time obviously,' John said. 'One hopes it suggests Pollard's following up another lead.'

Richard, less guarded, remarked that one couldn't help thinking about that Ash bloke at Hob's Cottage.

'For God's sake don't make remarks like that outside these four walls,' his father replied. 'Bringing slander and libel actions seems a popular pastime these days. And a damn profitable one.'

The united efforts of Rose, Henrietta and two of the daily women from Buckford produced an excellent celebration supper on a charmingly decorated table. John insisted on champagne and the atmosphere was festive. The bride-to-be's reply when toasted evoked a crescendo of applause.

'Thank you all for having me,' she said. 'Especially Adrian.'

'Obvious afterthought,' her future husband protested.

Later, over coffee in the library, the topic of the traffic census on the road below came up.

'What on earth's the idea?' Richard asked. 'There's next to no traffic.'

'Apparently the powers that be think it's on the increase and the narrowness and bends in the road are potentially dangerous,' John Morley replied.

'As long as they don't turn it into a motorway,' Gail said.

During the afternoon Toye had expressed a more appreciative attitude to motorways as the Rover headed for Brinkleigh.

'You get there on a road like this,' he commented while sweeping ahead of two cars in the fast lane.

They arrived at Brinkleigh just after 4 o'clock. An appointment had been made for Pollard with Mr Walter Ripley, of Swan, Ripley & Cornhill, and after clocking in at the Fox and Hounds, the little town's main hostelry, they arrived at 4.30 at the firm's office.

As they were shown into his room Walter Ripley got up from his desk to greet them.

'I'm delighted to meet you in person, Chief Superintendent,' he said, extending a welcoming hand. 'I've followed several of your cases in *The Times* with great interest. Do sit down, both of you. What can I do for you?'

'Our visit is connected with a client of yours, a Mr Stephen Ash,' replied Pollard, who had taken an immediate liking to the quiet grey-haired solicitor with shrewd eyes. 'We are hoping that you may be able to give us some help. We are on what has turned out to be a very difficult case of murder in Buckford and we think that Mr Ash may be involved. What do you know of him?'

'This firm drew up a will for his late great-aunt, Mrs Clara Firth, a rather eccentric old lady who died in old age last autumn in a nursing home in Cranforth, about 20 miles from here. She left everything she died possessed of to her great nephew Stephen Ash. He had emigrated to Australia after World War Two, and they were completely out of touch. Cutting a long story short, we succeeded in contacting him. He came over to see us, and after I had satisfied myself that he really was Stephen Ash — with the help of the Australian police, I may say — I handed over the legacy Mrs Firth had left him. He settled our account, and the firm has had no further contact with him.'

'I hope you may be able to help,' Pollard replied, 'and I'll be as concise as I can. The case is one in which the lie of the land plays a very important part, and Inspector

134

Toye — who is map-minded — has produced this sketch-map showing the setting of the murder of Miss Emily Gover, for 30 years employed by Mr and Mrs Morley of Glade Manor, first as nurse and later as housekeeper.' As he spoke he handed the map to Mr Ripley. 'Glade Manor and the Dower House are occupied by Mr John Morley and his second wife Rose, and by his son and daughter-in-law, Richard and Gail Morley. Both these houses are about half way up a wooded slope leading to a crest followed at a safe distance by a footpath. Beyond the crest the ridge drops sharply to a valley and Manor Farm. At one point on this sharp slope the ridge has been quarried for building stone. It was in this quarry that Emily Gover's body was found with that of the family dog, an elderly retriever. Is this clear so far, Mr Ripley?'

'Admirably. Please carry on.'

'You will see that the Manor and the Dower House are approached by a branching drive leading off a fairly minor road which crosses the little River Weaving and its valley by a low bridge. On the opposite side of the river is Hob's Cottage, a small place which was bought by Stephen Ash a couple of months ago, and which he is now restoring. Flat stepping stones make it possible to cross the Weaving unless the river is abnormally high after rain. Hob's Cottage was clearly part of the Glade Manor estate at one time. I should add, to complete the picture, that John Morley has a stepson, Adrian, adopted by him and his first wife, Fenella. Adrian is 31, and already a Reader in Classical Archaeology at Athanasius College, Oxford. Emily Gover was nanny to both Adrian and the slightly younger Richard before she became housekeeper to John and his first wife, Fenella ... All right, so far, Mr Ripley?'

'Perfectly. Please continue. It's absorbing.'

'On to Easter Monday, then,' Pollard said.

He moved concisely from the sudden falling in love of Adrian Morley and Henrietta Legge to the events of the following day. Adrian leaves early, hoping to get some time alone with Henrietta, but neighbours who are friends of both of them make this impossible. He returns to Oxford and rings Miss Gover to say that he has left some papers behind and will return to collect them on the following morning. Meanwhile all four Morleys are at a distant wedding. Adrian arrives early the next day and takes the family dog up to the top of the ridge while his breakfast is being cooked, and is seen by a Manor Farm worker. At about 10.30 he is seen driving through Buckford, but on arriving at Henrietta's cottage in Loxford finds that she has gone out, presumably to lunch. He drives to Heathrow, spends the night in a hotel, and leaves by plane for Ephesus early on Thursday morning. Meanwhile Richard and Gail Morley return to the Dower House on Wednesday evening. Gail rings Miss Gover before lunch on Thursday but gets no answer, and assumes she is out in the vegetable garden. At about 4.30 John and Rose Morley return home, and find no sign of Miss Gover in the house. Her body is discovered by John and Richard at the foot of the quarry below the crest of the ridge.

'At this point,' Pollard went on, 'we unfortunately started barking up the wrong tree. With some excuse, I think. The position was still that no witness had come forward who had seen Miss Gover alive after 10.30 on Wednesday morning when Adrian went off in his car. When we learnt that John Morley had managed to contact him at Ephesus and that he had said he was returning we had some qualms, but could not make out why he was allowing so much time for getting from Heathrow to Glade Manor. Inspector Toye is an absolutely first-class driver, and we tailed Adrian from

136

Heathrow to — you've got there, I'm sure, Mr Ripley — Miss Legge's cottage, virtually interrupting a proposal of marriage.'

Walter Ripley chuckled.

'Best story I've heard in years,' he said. 'Do carry on.'

'I will,' Pollard said. 'Actually it gets even better. The following day, feeling that we simply must get on to some other line or return to the AC with our tails between our legs we decided to search Miss Gover's flatlet at Glade Manor ourselves, although the local lads had been through it already. Our final effort was to take up a bit of the carpet. Underneath we found a cellophane envelope containing a sheet of newspaper dated July 1944 and containing a photograph of the first Mrs John Morley and a notice of her marriage to Bombardier Stephen Ash. Research at St Catherine's House revealed that the marriage was never dissolved. Stephen Ash emigrated, and Fenella went through the marriage ceremony with John Morley and produced Richard.'

'Good God!' Leaning back in his chair and contemplating Pollard and Toye with undisguised admiration, Mr Ripley asked what he could do to help.

'We are anxious to know how Ash got the information of Fenella Plume's marriage to John Morley, which opened up such a promising prospect of blackmail. Presumably you handed over various possessions of his great aunt's to him as well as his legacy? Can you possibly remember if, for instance, there were any letters among them?'

'I can't be as specific as that,' Walter Ripley said, 'but I definitely handed over a rather grotty suitcase that the nursing home sent along. The obvious thing is for me to put you in touch with the matron. I just opened it to show Stephen Ash, and remember that it was very neatly packed. He took it off with him. I'll ring the matron now.'

An appointment was arranged for 8.30 at the nursing home, and after thanking Walter Ripley for his help and promising to keep in touch Pollard and Toye returned to the Fox and Hounds for a much needed meal.

The Nightingale Nursing Home was on the outskirts of Cranforth, a small town about 20 miles from Brinkleigh. Its appearance suggested a high standard of maintenance with correspondingly high fees. Pollard and Toye were shown into the matron's private sitting room. She was a small middle-aged woman who gave the impression of brisk kindly competence and considerable interest in their visit.

'I can't imagine that I can be of any help to you,' she told Pollard, 'but of course I'll give you any information about the late Mrs Firth that I can. I only took over this nursing home five years ago so know very little about her past history. She came to us because her health was failing — she was 88 — and died very peacefully after a couple of years. Not as the result of pneumonia or any specific illness. She just faded out.'

'Did she have many visitors?'

'Very few. She seemed a very solitary person with a great-nephew in Australia as her only surviving relative and had lost touch with him. A few kind-hearted local people looked in from time to time and the vicar called once a month, but otherwise there was nobody.'

'What about letters?'

'As far as I can remember she never received anything that looked like a personal letter in my time. Anything that was obviously a business letter was sent on to her local solicitor, Mr Hargreaves.'

'Who arranged her funeral and so on?'

'Mr Hargreaves, but it turned out that her Will and everything arising from it was in the hands of Swan, Ripley & Cornhill, a firm of solicitors in Brinkleigh, as

138

you know. An unusual arrangement, but she was very close about her private affairs.'

'I suppose,' Pollard said, 'Mrs Firth had a few personal belongings with her here?'

'Very few,' the matron replied. 'She had sold up her house and almost everything in it. She brought just one suitcase with a supply of nightdresses and so forth, a few books and some old-fashioned jewellery, and just a few oddments. These things were packed and sent on to Swan, Ripley & Cornhill who were her executors.'

'Can you remember if there were any letters among the oddments?'

'Yes, there were. A packet of about two dozen. The poor old lady used to read them through until she got past it.'

'Did she ever talk about who they had been from, and say anything about what was in them?'

'Only that they were from old friends giving news of people they had both known, Superintendent. Mrs Firth was exceedingly close about her past and her affairs generally.'

The essential fact had been established and there was obiviously nothing more to be learnt from the Nightingale Nursing Home. After a little discreet conversation about the case Pollard managed to extricate Toye and himself and they returned to Brinkleigh to stay the night at the Fox and Hounds.

'Bed for me,' said Pollard over a drink, 'and a fairly early start tomorrow morning. We haven't really picked up much, but the fact that old Mrs Firth's collection of personal letters was handed over to Ash could possibly explain how he got on to Fenella's trail.'

He woke the next morning to find a query had taken shape in his mind, and put it to Toye at breakfast.

'That legacy that Ash got from his great-aunt,' he said,

'Ripley said he handed it over to him. What did he mean exactly? Unless it were a mere few pounds, surely it must have been a cheque or some share certificates? If so, what did Ash do next? I'll ring up Ripley and find out.'

After swallowing a second cup of coffee he went off to telephone to Mr Ripley. Toye finished his breakfast and waited in the hall until Pollard emerged from the telephone kiosk.

'We could be on to something,' he said. 'Ripley says he contacted the manager of the local branch of the Northern Counties Bank, and made an appointment for Ash to go along and make a temporary arrangement to deposit his legacy there. It was about thirty thousand, apparently. We'll go and see if we can get anything out of the chap.'

It was a small branch and on Pollard's presenting his official card they were shown into the manager's room within minutes. He was a young and alert-looking man and recalled his dealings with Mr Stephen Ash without hesitation.

'On my advice Mr Ash deposited the whole sum with us, less £800 to finance a return trip to Sydney and settle up his affairs there, and it was clearly understood that when he had chosen a place for retirement somewhere nearer the south of England the money would be withdrawn and transferred to a bank there. This took place a couple of months ago, to the Southern Counties Bank, in a place called Brading.'

'Thanks,' Pollard said. 'That's perfectly clear. And since then, presumably you haven't had any further contact with him?'

'None at all. Incidentally a man called here about a couple of weeks ago asking if we could give him Mr Ash's address, as they had been friends in Sydney and he wanted to meet up with him again. I said that I hadn't got the address, and suggested that he wrote to Mr Ash c/o his bank and they would forward it. After all, Mr Ash mightn't have wanted to continue the contact.'

'Quite,' Pollard replied. 'Was the man an Australian, by the way?'

'Either an Australian born or an Englishman who'd lived out there for a long time,' the bank manager replied.

Outside on the pavement Pollard hesitated briefly.

'You know, Toye,' he said, 'once again I think there's a faint whiff of fish. You haven't encountered Ash yourself, but personally I simply can't imagine anybody being such a pal of his that he'd go to the trouble of trying to contact him over here while ostensibly on holiday ... I think I'll contact Bosworth and ask him to step up the manpower at Glade if he possibly can.'

They made good time on the return to London and arrived at the Yard in the early afternoon. Pollard was informed that Mr John Morley had rung, urgently requesting him to contact him as soon as he got back. A call was sent through at once.

'Sorry not to have been available earlier on,' he told John Morley. 'I was following up a lead north. Some trouble at your end?'

'No, not trouble. It could be useful information. Nanky was seen about mid-day on the Thursday of her murder. Before Easter I ordered some white paint for one of our greenhouses. I always get my paint from Little's of Gilland, a town about the size of Brading but in the opposite direction, seven miles to the west. Understandably in the light of what happened when my wife and I got home on that Thursday I never gave the paint a thought, but yesterday I came on the cans in a shed behind the house. One of them was holding down a note left by the delivery man. It was on a piece of paper and said "No one in so have left paint here as can see Nanky coming over stones from Hob. She'll see it and put tins in. Harry for Littles. 12.10 Thursday." Here it is.'

'Definitely useful,' Pollard commented, after reading it. 'I happen to know that Harry went on to deliver paint at Hob's Cottage. Incidentally, Mr Adrian Morley was seen driving through Buckford an hour and half earlier, wasn't he? Have you taken any steps to contact Harry?'

'No. I thought I'd better hand over to you when you got back.'

'Quite right. Will you contact Little's and say that Harry is wanted as a witness as he saw Nanky that morning. I'm coming down myself tomorrow and will take a statement from him. I'd better go straight to Little's before coming on to you. Is their place easy to find?'

'It's a big shop in the main street. You can't miss it.'

'Right. Is the traffic census operating all right?'

'Yes, thanks. We've also acquired a retriever pup to take poor old Tim's place. I'll be at the Manor all day tomorrow.'

Pollard rang off and turned his attention to the report on Stephen Ash from the police authorities in Sydney. It stated that during his early days in New South Wales he had lived fairly rough, getting what casual jobs he could pick up and being involved in a few brawls and being pulled in, but dismissed with cautions. As time went on he had obtained regular work connected with building, acquired skills and gradually became a small-scale property owner, forming a partnership with a George Rendell, who, as already reported, had recently left Sydney. A few years earlier both men had been charged with fraud in connection with house building but the charge against Ash had been dismissed on grounds of insufficient evidence. Rendell had served two years in

142

prison and been released in the previous summer, but the partnership had not been renewed and relations between him and Ash were noticeably cool. His present whereabouts were unknown, but he had left a deposit in his bank account and presumably intended to return to Sydney.

The Assistant Commissioner listened with interest to Pollard's account of his visit to Brinkleigh.

'You'd better go down to the Brading area again tomorrow,' he said. 'As I see it, you're in a strong enough position to charge Ash with Emily Gover's murder, now that you've got that van driver's evidence of having seen her coming away from Hob's Cottage at midday on the Wednesday she was killed. The nursing home matron's evidence about that packet of letters is suggestive, and I expect he learnt about Fenella's marriage to John Morley from one of them. No proof, of course, but a distinct possibility. He might even admit it under questioning.'

Pollard agreed.

'I can't see any prospect of more direct evidence,' he said.

'Right then,' the AC replied. 'Good hunting.'

Harry Banks, the van driver from Little's, who delivered paint on the day of the murder to Glade Manor was a small alert man obviously thrilled at being interviewed by a Chief Superintendent of Scotland Yard.

'Did you know Miss Gover well?' Pollard asked him.

'Sure I did, sir. I've been delivering paint and suchlike to Glade Manor twenty year or more. I took that last lot round the back, like I always did, but I couldn't get no answer. So I went round to the front to find out if anyone was home. Nobody came when I rang the bell, and as I turned round on the top of the steps to go back and put a note with the paint I saw Miss Gover pickin' her way back from 'Obs over the steppin' stones. I was a bit late on me round so I didn't wait for 'er. Just wrote a bit of a note and drove off in me van.'

'Would you,' Pollard said, 'be willing to swear that the woman you saw on the stepping stones was Miss Gover?'

'That I would, sir. Take me Bible oath. From up on the top of the front door steps you looks over the trees and right across the river.'

'Inspector Toye here will write out a statement of what you've told us and ask you to read it carefully. If you agree that it's an accurate record, are you prepared to sign it?'

'I am, sir. I'd like to feel I helped cop the brute who did Miss Gover.'

After a quick lunch Pollard and Toye drove to Glade Manor. As they drew up at the front door John Morley appeared at the top of the steps.

'Come along in,' he said. 'Bosworth's here, and wants to see you. Harry Banks turned up all right, I hope?'

'He was waiting for us, all agog, and a most sensible witness,' Pollard replied as they were escorted to John Morley's study. 'So a really vital piece of information's now in the bag thanks to that purchase of cans of paint.'

Inspector Bosworth was clearly relieved at Pollard's arrival.

'I've been in two minds about whether I ought to have taken any steps or not,' he said, 'but it's your case, not mine, Super, so I've held my hand beyond stepping up the spoof traffic census a bit. The night before last — Thursday night, that was — the young chap I'd put on the job had something in his report. About 4 o'clock there was a noise quite near at hand. A mixture of a splash and a thud, he said. Just the one noise, nothing further. He went straight to the gate of Hob's Cottage and crept along the edge of the grass, right up to the house itself, but there wasn't a sound from inside. He waited a bit, went down to have a look at the river, and then came away again.'

'He didn't go round to the back?'

'Impossible,' he said, 'without making a hell of a racket. There's a grotty corrugated iron fence with a door in it.'

'What happened yesterday?'

'Nothing out of the ordinary. Ash was about the place, putting up a new gutter most of the time. He didn't go out at all, my chaps said. This morning he got his car out early and fiddled with the engine a bit, and finally went off about a quarter to ten. To the races at Westingham was a pretty safe guess. He goes to pretty well all the meetings apparently, and there's one today. I got on to the Westingham Super and he sent a couple of chaps to check the car parks. He rang back just before I left Brading to say Ash's car is in one of them.'

'Believe me,' Pollard said, 'the co-operation we've had from you Brading people over this case won't be forgotten.'

He took a step towards the window and stood for a moment looking out. John Morley's study was at the back of the house and the beginning of the track up through the woods went past it. Emily Gover and the old retriver had gone this way to their deaths.

'In nearly all my cases,' he said, turning back to Toye and Inspector Bosworth, 'there seems to be a moment when one knows it's time to get up and go, and this is it. I've got the warrant, and we know Ash is over at Westingham. There's plenty of cover at Hob's Cottage: the garage, another shed and a hedge, and we'll be there when he comes back and pull him in. But he's obviously a violent man, and although Toye and I were issued with guns at the Yard this morning I think we could do with some extra manpower. Could you rustle up a couple of hefty chaps, Inspector? What about calling off the traffic census? That would give us one extra?'

A sense of action took over. Inspector Bosworth rang the Brading police station and reported that a further reinforcement was leaving for Glade Manor immediately. Toye would wait for his arrival and bring him to Hob's Cottage by way of the stepping stones over the Weaving. Pollard would drive Inspector Bosworth down to the 'traffic census' post, collect the constable on duty, leave the Yard car there and then go on to the cottage on foot.

Ten minutes later the Rover drew up at the 'traffic control' point. A young man in mufti stepped forward with notebook and biro, took one look at Inspector Bosworth as he got out of the car and saluted smartly. Pollard, getting out on the far side and locking the Rover, grinned at hearing the information about himself that was being given to the constable. A moment later he was receiving an even more impressive salute.

'Lock up here and follow on, Willis,' Bosworth said. 'You're in luck. There's going to be a job on.'

He led the way with Pollard.

In a couple of minutes they turned into the drive of Hob's Cottage and made their way to the untidy open space in front of the little house. Pollard looked at his watch.

'Inspector Toye and A.N. Other can't possibly get here under an hour,' he said. 'In the meantime I'd just like to put Constable Willis in the picture, and then we'll have a good look round from the point of view of cover for when Ash turns up. Those planks over there aren't too bad to sit on ... Now then, Constable Willis, you're genned up on the local murder, I'm sure: Miss Emily

146

Gover, employed at Glade Manor over there, who was thrown over the edge of a quarry.'

'Yessir.' The young man's eyes were riveted upon Pollard, his expression one of incredulous gratification at the situation in which he had suddenly found himself.

'Well, the position now is that we've got enough evidence to pull him in when he comes back from the Westingham races. Ash is a violent man and will almost certainly resist when I charge him. It'll be a case of moving in like lightning, grabbing his arms and pinioning them behind him. We don't know if he'll drive straight into the shed he uses for a garage or pull up outside the cottage door. Let's have a look at what cover there is while we're waiting for Inspector Toye and the extra chap he's bringing back from your place.'

'Sir.'

'Yes?'

'Will Ash have a gun?'

'Quite possibly. Inspector Toye and I were issued with them this morning. But quick action when we move in is what I'm aiming at.'

The garage itself and various shrubs provided cover, but the most useful discovery was that the door in the decrepit corrugated iron fence, stretching from the cottage to the garden wall behind the garage, was unlocked. Its hinges were ill-fitting, and if the door was kept marginally ajar, anyone behind it had a clear view of the whole courtyard.

'The Yard car,' Pollard said suddenly. 'Inspector Toye's going to park it a short distance up the Manor drive, and then come on here.'

A powerful car went past, slowed suddenly and the engine was switched off. Within five minutes Toye arrived with a hefty young man in uniform who turned out to be a contemporary of Constable Willis. Pollard

147

went over the agreed strategy for Ash's arrival, and a minor variation proposed by Toye was adopted.

'Well, that about sums it up, I think,' he said, glancing at his watch. 'We can relax *pro tem*, but action stations if there's the faintest sound of a car approaching. I don't expect Ash will turn up for at least another hour. Smoke if you want to.'

After a chat with Toye and Bosworth, Pollard strolled about in the courtyard, appearing to contemplate his surroundings with interest. He was experiencing the tension which always gripped him as the zero hour of making the arrest drew on. He stood contemplating the front of the cottage, speculating as to its date and trying to make out the crudely carved lettering over the door. Moving on, he found himself approaching the overgrown disused well that he had noticed on his earlier visit. As his eyes fell on it he registered a sudden violent shock. The bindweed was limp, withered and largely dead. Bending to investigate it more closely he saw that most of it had been roughly cut through at its roots round the greater part of the well cover.

'Here, will you?' he heard himself call with an abrupt urgency that brought Toye, Bosworth and the two constables to his side in seconds.

He explained the situation in a few brief sentences.

'Why, I haven't got a clue, but I've got a hunch that this cover's simply got to come up,' he ended.

The hefty young constable from Brading stepped forward.

'May I have a go, sir?'

Without waiting for an answer he knelt on the stonework rim of the wall, gripped the iron ring in the centre of the wooden cover and gave a series of powerful heaves.

The cover came up at last and he pushed it out of the

way. Moved by a common impulse the five men crowded round the mouth of the well shaft. There was a moment of dead silence followed by a variety of expletives.

Pollard automatically assumed command of the situation.

'Ladder,' he ordered. 'The one against the cottage. It may be long enough.'

'In God's name who's the bloke down there?' Inspector Bosworth asked.

'Could be a bloke from Sydney from some information I've had from the police out there,' Pollard replied abstractedly while watching the ladder being lowered into the well. 'A George Rendell. Once a partner of Ash's. Ladder's just possible from the look of it. Tow rope from the boot of the car, don't you think, Toye?'

Ted Willis tentatively mentioned that he was a pot-holer and was allowed to make the descent. The dead man's head and shoulders were above the water level, and the rope was quickly and efficiently secured round his waist and shoulders. It took the united efforts of all five men to hoist him to the surface. It was obvious that the initial cause of death had been a violent blow shattering his skull.

'We've got to step on it,' Pollard said as he wiped the sweat from his face. 'We'll get the poor devil round to the back of the garage. Bosworth, you're obviously the chap to get local help. I suggest you take the Rover and beat it up to the Manor to ring your Super at Brading for support. Get it across that it's urgent. We'll cope here and only hope that you'll get back before Ash turns up. Meanwhile we'll clear up what we can of the mess here. It's vital that Ash shouldn't spot what's happened until he's out of his car and we can grab him. Get the well-cover back, you young chaps,' he ordered as Bosworth roard off.

The well-cover was heavy and the two constables had a struggle to get it into position. At last it sealed the well head with a thud. Meanwhile Pollard and Toye searched the body of the drowned man only to find that all traces of identity had been removed from the sodden clothing. All the pockets were empty, and the makers' names had been cut out of the garments. There were no shoes.

'We'll get the poor blighter behind the garage,' Pollard said. 'Thank the Lord I can hear Bosworth starting up the car over at the Manor. With any luck he'll be back here before Ash turns up.'

In the event Bosworth parked his car just inside the drive gates of the Manor and got back to the scene of action before there was any sign of Stephen Ash's return. Pollard had meanwhile assigned concealed vantage points to his support. Barely two tense minutes had elapsed before the sound of a car coming from the direction of Buckford became audible. Almost at once Ash's Fiesta turned in at the gate. He drove straight up the rough drive into the open garage. A brief pause elapsed before he heaved himself out of the car, slammed the door and began to stride towards the cottage. Then, suddenly registering the wet and disordered grass round the well, he froze in his tracks. Synchronising perfectly with his exit from the garage the two constables came round the corners of the building and gripped his forearms while Toye handcuffed his wrists behind his back. Uttering a steam of oaths he found himself confronted by Pollard. There was a sudden dramatic silence.

'Stephen Ash,' Pollard said, 'I charge you with the murder of . . . . '

'I never killed the old hag,' Ash shouted. 'The bloody dog pulled her over the edge, so I cleared out.'

'I charge you,' Pollard repeated slowly and clearly, 'with the murder of a person unknown whose body we have just recovered from the well over there. I also charge you,' he continued, 'with the murder of Miss Emily Gover by forcing her over the edge of the quarry on the Glade Manor estate. The jury will take note of the fact that the prints of the dog's claws were over and not under her footprints in a patch of mud at the edge of the quarry.'

It took four of the five detectives present to get Stephen Ash into the Rover *en route* for Brading police station.

After Stephen Ash had arrived at the police station and been formally charged with the murders of Emily Gover and an unknown person of the male sex he was lodged in a cell overnight, and informed that he would appear before the Brading magistrates on the following Monday morning.

Pollard, struggling with exhaustion, asked the telephone operator to put him through to Glade Manor.

'Superintendent Pollard here, Mr Morley,' he said when John Morley answered the call. 'I'm ringing to tell you that Stephen Ash has just been charged with the murder of Emily Gover. He is in police custody here at Brading, and will appear before the magistrates on Monday morning at 11 o'clock, and we can take it that he'll be committed for trial at the Assizes. Incidentally, he faces a second murder charge: a man's body was found by us in the disused well at Hob's Cottage.'

'Another man's body?' John Morley repeated in a bemused voice.

'Yes. I take it, Mr Morley, that you'll be attending the committal proceedings?'

'Well, I suppose I ought to.'

'As Miss Gover's employer for the past 30 years it would be expected, I think. You're bound to be involved

151

in the case to some extent, I'm afraid. I'll see that a place is kept for you. Good night, Mr Morley.'

John Morley was to discover to his dismay that attendance at Stephen Ash's committal proceedings was only the first of numerous dealings with the police on the subject of Nanky's life history. They questioned him minutely on any contacts with the outside world that she had made during her time at Glade Manor. In addition, work had to go on at Morley's Book Restoration. He was also grimly determined to get possession of Hob's Cottage and have it razed to the ground, the well filled in and covered over, and the site planted with trees. Negotiations for the purchase were time-consuming.

Rose Morley had developed a warm affection for Nanky, but the emotional link with her was less strong than that of the other members of the family. During the distressing publicity which had to be endured during the lengthy enquiries leading up to Stephen Ash's trial, she concentrated on supporting her husband. Considerable effort was needed to keep the Manor's domestic routine running smoothly, and it took several months to find a tolerable replacement for Nanky.

The aftermath of the tragedy involved Richard and Gail at a deeper and more personal level. Coming back from the Works one evening he found her in tears in an armchair in their sitting room.

'Darling, what is it?' he asked, dropping on to his knees beside her. 'Feeling rotten? Sick?'

'No. Nothing like that.' She buried her face in his coat.

'What then? Tell me.'

'It's — it's that I knew.'

'Knew what?'

'About your Mum and Stephen Ash.'

'Do you mean that somehow you came to know that Dad and my Mum weren't legally married?' Richard asked in astonishment.

Gail stared at him in equal amazement.

'But *you* knew?' She asked with a little gasp.

'Yes. You see, she told Dad about Ash before she died. Afterwards he told me and Adrian. And how in heaven's name did you come to know about it?'

She took his hand and held it tightly.

'It was the day I went up to St Catherine's House about some searches. I heard Stephen Ash getting the certificate of his marriage to Fenella Plume, so I knew there couldn't have been a divorce. And when he turned up at Hob's Cottage it stood out a mile that he'd somehow got on to your Mum's and Dad's marriage, and obviously came to make trouble, among other things. I just didn't know what to do for the best, and put off a decision until after Easter and while we all went up to the wedding. And when we got back and the murder had happened I felt sure that Nanky had somehow found out about Ash, and told him to clear out or she'd go to your Dad herself about what he was planning to do.'

Richard held her very close.

'Darling love,' he said, 'I just can't bear to think of how dreadfully unhappy you've been, and absolutely no reason for it. Dad had me officially legitimated after Mum died. So you're not married to a bastard, and little Theophilus won't have an illegitimate father. Perhaps I ought to have told you about it, but Dad has always been so very anxious that it shouldn't leak out, and Adrian and I gave him our solemn word that we'd keep it to ourselves. Of course Mum was wrong not to tell Dad: a divorce could easily have been arranged for her.'

'But Richard, why didn't she tell your father all about it?'

'I know it seems incomprehensible,' he said thoughtfully, 'but I understand it better now that I'm older. As a person Mum was a mixture of strength of character and sensitiveness. She'd got off in life to a poor start, losing both parents as a young child and being taken over by an apparently unimaginative aunt. Being called up and going into the ATS in the war brought out her strong side and gave her confidence. She did well and got promotion. She was easy on the eye, you know, and while she was in the ATS she unfortunately met Ash, who fell for her and agreed to give in to her scruples and get married. They were basically incompatible, of course, and he was soon tired of her and going off with other women. After about 18 months he announced that he was pushing off for good. Emigrating, and she'd never see or hear anything of him again. No point in wasting cash over a divorce.'

'Did she go to pieces completely?'

'No. The strong side of her came uppermost. She was quite alone and had to fend for herself. She had her gratuity, of course, and managed to get a job in Harridges. Dad happened to go in one day and fell for her at first sight. You can imagine the contrast he was to that bounder, Ash. Mum hesitated for a bit, afraid she'd lose him if he knew about Ash, and finally couldn't resist accepting him, both for what he was and what he had to offer her. The wrong decision, of course, but so much happiness came out of it ... We all loved her so.'

'I know I should have, too.' Gail said.

They sat in silence for a few moments holding hands. Then Richard gave her another kiss and got to his feet.

'By the way, there's something else off several people's chests today,' he told her. 'The Manderville *Decameron*. Its restoration's finished and it looks absolutely super.

The chap's coming down to collect it tomorrow. I'll run you over to the Works to have a look at it.'

Gail gave a delighted exclamation with a sense of skies clearing overhead.

The relationship between Adrian and Nanky had always been closer than that of the other members of the Morley family, much though she was loved by them. Adrian's grief at her tragic death had been more acute than John's or Richard's, and obviously more so than Rose's who had only known her for a comparatively short time. But in its keenest form Adrian's sense of loss had been abruptly overtaken by his sudden and unforeseen falling in love with Henrietta Legge. Nanky withdrew, as it were, to the background of his consciousness, but her place there was assured. During the hectic weeks of house-hunting in Oxford he often found himself assessing domestic possibilities with an echo of her robust common sense, and found this warming and even amusing.

The wedding took place in the early summer. It was a small, quiet one followed by a reception at Glade Manor for intimate friends. The location of the honeymoon had been kept a secret from everyone but the Morleys. With final embraces from John and Rose, the newly-wedded pair set off down the familiar drive and turned left into the Buckford road. As they passed Hob's Cottage they did not notice it.

Chapter 9

Pollard had regretfully declined the invitation to the
wedding on account of the heavy workload involved in
the investigation of two murders: Emily Gover's and that
of the man whose body had been found in the well of
Hob's Cottage. While convinced that the latter was
George Rendell, conclusive proof was not so far forthcoming. Stephen Ash had appeared before the Brading
magistrates, charged with both murders, and the case
had been adjourned because of insufficient evidence for
committal. Pollard had been provided with an office at
Brading police station and was engaged in paperwork
with Toye one morning when Superintendent Loosemore
looked in and enquired how things were going.

'You oughtn't to have much trouble over the Gover
case,' he said, 'what with her footprints and the dog's
claw marks going over the edge and Ash's behind them.'

'I'm not all that confident,' Pollard said, stretching
and clasping his hands behind his head. 'Can't you hear
counsel for the defence explaining to the jury how Gover
had obviously slipped on the mud while admiring the
view and dragged the dog after her? And how a chap had
come along a bit later and stood gaping at the prints and
wondering if there'd been an accident? And so far no one
has come forward to say they saw Ash anywhere near the

Glade Manor grounds on that Wednesday afternoon. Then the next thing ... Come in,' he called in response to a knock on the door.

'Excuse me, sir,' a Brading sergeant reported, 'there's a Buckford woman who's turned up with a couple of kids. She says she's got some information about the Glade Manor woods case and won't give it to anyone but you.'

Pollard groaned.

'What do you make of her, Sergeant? Sensation-monger? Trying to get herself into the papers?'

'I wouldn't say either of those, sir. Sensible sort of woman I'd call her.'

'Well, we'd better see her I suppose, Toye. Lead on, Sergeant. Thanks for looking in, Super. We'll keep in touch.'

They were conducted to a small waiting room where a youngish woman and two boys of roughly eight and ten years of age were sitting rather uneasily at an ink-stained wooden table. Pollard placed the woman as working-class in her early 30s, and noted corn-coloured hair, a fresh complexion, and a determined expression. The boys, although rather overawed, looked alert. All three were meticulously neat in appearance. The sergeant introduced the party as Mrs Crofter of Buckford and her sons, and withdrew.

'Good afternoon, Mrs Crofter,' Pollard said as he and Toye sat down, facing the group. 'I understand you've some information for us to do with the late Miss Gover's death?'

'That's right, sir,' she replied. ''tis the boys, really, and their Dad and I think as you ought to 'ear it. 'E'd 'ave come 'imself but 'e's on the railway and workin' on a job up the line, so I've kept the two of 'em out of school and brought 'em along. 'Twas the Wednesday —'

157

'Just a minute, Mrs Crofter,' Pollard broke in. 'We'll first have your names and address.'

This information having been noted by Toye, Mrs Crofter was invited to go ahead.

'Twas the Wednesday that the poor lady went over into the quarry, sir. Soon as the boys were off the school bus they came in for a bite, same as they always do, and went off on their bikes. We 'as tea at 6 near enough, soon as me 'usband gets in. The boys says —'

'I wonder,' Pollard interrupted, 'if they could tell me themselves where they went and what they did? You're Tommy, aren't you?' he asked the elder boy.

'Yessir. 'Twas this way. Pete and I went out on the Glade road. Just as you come to 'Ob's Cottage the road goes a bit downhill and round a corner to the gate, an' if you've got up a bit o' speed and the gates open you goes right in. 'Twas open, and we 'ad several goes. There wasn't no sign o' the man as lives there, so us thought 'e must be out.'

'But 'e weren't,' took up the younger boy. 'All of a suddin 'e came runnin' out o' the cottage, shakin' 'is fist an' yellin' at us. 'E called us —'

'That'll do,' Mrs Crofter cut in hastily. 'We don't want no rude words 'ere.'

'What did you do then?' Pollard asked the boys.

'Went back 'ome for tea.'

'Well, get on,' Mrs Crofter urged. 'Tell the gentlemen what 'appened when you went there next time, as you didn't orter 'ave done.'

During the next ten minutes Pollard concentrated on piecing together a somewhat disjointed narrative of unexpected interest. It appeared that on the Wednesday of Emily Gover's death the school attended by the Crofter boys had an unexpected half-holiday on account of some building work on the premises. They had come

158

home to dinner and afterwards gone out on their bicycles with firm instructions to keep out of mischief and be back in good time for tea. They had, however, made a provisional plan of action which they kept to themselves. Tommy had purloined a piece of white chalk from school, and they set off to find out if the man at Hob's Cottage was at home or had gone off in his car somewhere. This proved to be the case, both the gate and the garage door being open. They had gone up the short rough drive, prospected cautiously, and finally decided that the coast was clear. Peter had kept guard while Tommy inscribed a number of unflattering epithets on the front door. At a sudden warning gesture from Peter they dropped on all fours and crawled to a gap in the hedge overlooking the Weaver valley. Stephen Ash was crossing the Weaver by the stepping stones, and on reaching the far bank headed for the Manor Woods. The afternoon's fun had suddenly taken an even more exciting turn. They decided to trail their enemy, streaked along to the Manor gates, hid their bicycles in the hedge, and began to make their way as quietly as possible through the woods on the left side of the drive.

Then, without warning, the exciting adventure acquired a new and frightening character. There was a terrified scream from somewhere higher up the wooded slope. It was followed almost immediately by the sound of someone crashing through bushes and feet beginning to run down the drive with heavy pounding steps. The boys had scrambled for cover behind a clump of brambles, Peter tearing his T-shirt in the process. The steps came nearer and nearer, and peering out through a gap in the brambles they had seen the Hob's Cottage man go past, gasping for breath. He abruptly slowed down on reaching the drive gate, and they could hear him walking along the road towards his cottage. Creeping out of their cover they crossed the drive and watched the man's progress along the road and finally into the Hob's gate which he slammed behind him. Without waiting to watch his reactions to the inscriptions on his front door they retrieved their bicycles and rode off to the right, making for home by a route avoiding Hob's Cottage altogether.

Their arrival home had been overclouded by Mrs Crofter's indignation at the tear in Peter's brand new T-shirt, and the frightening scream and the hasty departure of the Hob's Cottage man from the Glade Manor woods began to loom less in their minds as the days passed. But they were intelligent boys and Tommy was old enough to feel a certain sense of responsibility. At long last they blurted out the story of their experience to their horrified parents with the result that they were taken to Brading to tell the Scotland Yard man all about it.

When he was satisfied that he was in full possession of the facts Pollard sat reflecting for some moments.

'Mrs Crofter,' he said at last, 'it was absolutely right of you to bring the boys to tell me about what happened to them that Wednesday afternoon. It may be very important. I want all three of you to come with me right away to the Manor woods and go over the ground there. Inspector Toye will drive us in the police car, and afterwards we'll drop you off at your home. Are you willing to do this?'

The boys' eyes lit up at the exciting prospect of a drive in a Scotland Yard car, and after slight hesitation Mrs Crofter agreed. During the drive Tommy and Peter sat in front with Toye, bombarding him with questions about the Rover's engine and performance. Sitting in the back with Mrs Crofter, Pollard introduced topics about the family's home life and prospects. The journey passed quickly, and they parked outside the Glade Manor gates.

'Just show us exactly what you did,' Pollard told the

160

boys. In a few minutes the party had progressed through the woods to a point about a third of the way up to the top of the ridge.

'Just 'ere 'twas, sir,' Tommy said. 'Us 'eard the scream and just bolted into them brambles. See?' He pointed at the bushes where they had hidden.

Mrs Crofter suddenly burst into indignant speech.

'I'll say 'twas there! Look at that strip o' your brand new T-shirt, Peter, 'anging on the thorns.'

She made a movement to retrieve it, but Pollard checked her.

'I think we'll borrow that bit of T-shirt for a short time, Mrs Crofter,' he said. 'Perhaps when we drop you at your house you'd let us borrow what's left of that shirt too?'

She looked at him, comprehension slowly dawning in her eyes.

''Tis evidence they were 'ere as they says?'

'That's right, Mrs Crofter,' Pollard replied.

After they had called at the Crofters' home in Buckford, Toye reversed and drove back to Hob's Cottage. As the Rover drew up at the front door two members of the Brading police came out.

'Any luck?' Pollard asked.

'Nothing inside, sir,' the sergeant in charge of the search told him. 'But over there behind the shed where the car was kept we thought the ground had a look of being dug over. We had a go with a spade and found the turf had been lifted and put back careful-like, so as not to show. We got it up and there was a hole full of burnt stuff. Seeing as you was coming, Mr Pollard, we didn't touch nothing.'

'Lead me to it,' Pollard said, aware of a touch of excitement. Kneeling beside the hole he prodded cautiously with a stair rod. 'It's about a foot deep, so there must have been quite a bit of stuff burnt in it. Look here, I want to get the whole lot out, disturbing it as little as possible. It must be stuff connected with the bloke in the well. Any ideas, either of you?'

After some discussion they dug round the cavity leaving a layer of earth all around it. This they then enclosed in a strip of material torn off a ground sheet. Finally they worked a large spade under the estimated depth of the burnt matter and with the greatest care raised it and managed to transfer it to a bucket.

'Stout effort,' Pollard said, mopping his brow. 'All due to you chaps using your eyes. You may have pulled off something damned important. Inspector Toye and I are driving up to London tonight, and we'll dump this little lot in the science labs.'

No messages were waiting at Brading police station, and shortly afterwards the Rover was on the London road. On arrival at the Yard Toye handed over the box of charred fragments to the laboratory staff on duty amid the expected contumely, while Pollard went to his office to find that no response to his urgent enquiries about George Rendell had so far arrived from Sydney. Both men thankfully headed for their homes and a brief respite. It was nearly midnight as Pollard quietly opened the front door of his house in Wimbledon, but a light came from the kitchen and Jane emerged in her dressing gown.

'Meal ready if you want it,' she said. 'No need to talk if you're flat out. I'll retire to bed.'

'Stay if you can face it,' he said as he kissed her, 'but I warn you I'm simply ravenous.'

While making inroads into a steak and kidney pudding which had been simmering in the oven, Pollard brought her up to date on the latest developments in the case of the murder of Emily Gover.

'Well, I should think that's pretty well conclusive as far as Stephen Ash is concerned,' Jane said. 'You must be grateful to those Crofter kids and the handy bramble bush which tore the strip off the shirt of one of them.'

Pollard agreed. Work on preparing the Crown's case against Ash could now go ahead.

'But the business of the chap we yanked out of Stephen Ash's well is just a mass of loose ends at the moment,' he went on. 'I'm dead certain he's Rendell, Ash's former partner in Sydney, but his identity has got to be proved beyond any doubt before a really convincing case can be brought against Ash.'

'Have you had anything useful from the Sydney police yet?' Jane asked.

'So far, only that it's quite definite that Rendell was in Sydney after Ash's return visit last winter to settle up his affairs. He — Rendell — went away about a month after Ash came back here. Paid the rent of his flat for three months in advance and left a sizeable deposit in his bank. Gave out that he was going to see what building prospects were in Malaya.

Pollard pushed an empty plate away and yawned hugely.

'Bed for you, right now,' Jane said, collecting up used plates and cutlery. 'Have you got to be early at the Yard tomorrow?'

'Yes, dammit, because of the time difference. The chap who's on the job in Sydney is ringing me at about half past eight our time.'

On the following morning the call from Sydney came through on time. The enquiries about Ash and Rendell put in hand by the local police had already produced some useful information. Pollard learnt that when Ash had returned after going to England to claim his legacy he had been over the top.

'Bloody full of himself and his affairs,' the Sydney police officer in charge of the enquiries requested by Pollard reported. 'Shooting his mouth off about how he was clearing out for good and going back to put his feet up in the old country. Somewhere in the south where it would be decently warm most times. Near a racecourse. Ash was hooked on racing and never missed a good meeting out here!'

Pollard asked about recent relations between Ash and Rendell, and heard that they'd often met in popular pubs but they'd never been on the former friendly terms since Rendell's imprisonment. Quite a lot of folk thought he'd been forced to carry the can.

'Looks as though Ash had some hold on him, doesn't it?'

'Could be,' the Australian agreed. 'And that now Ash had come into money Rendell might have made up his mind to get his hands on some of it. Anyway, thought it was worth a trip to the UK to have a go. He may have had some sort of a hold on Ash. They were both run in the time Rendell copped it, but the charge against Ash couldn't be made to stick.'

'I suppose it's absolutely certain that Ash finally left Australia before Rendell took off?'

'Absolutely, Super. We've contacted quite a few folk who were in touch with Rendell after Ash had gone. He gave out that he was going to see if there were any promising openings in the building line in Malaya where various schemes have been discussed lately. And he meant to come back. Left some hundreds in the bank and paid three months' rent of his flat in advance.'

'What was the reaction in Sydney when the news about Ash being arrested on a murder charge came through?'

'Folk just didn't believe it at first, seeing how he'd gone on here about his legacy. Couldn't stop talking about how he was going to do himself bloody well. The general idea seems to be that he'd had a row with a bookie or somebody and hit the chap a bit too hard.'

'Well, thanks a lot for all this gen,' Pollard said. 'I'm most grateful. There doesn't seem to me to be any doubt that the chap in the well was Rendell but conclusive proof is what I'm out for. We'll be in touch.'

He rang off and sat for a couple of minutes deep in thoughts and plans. Then he called his secretary on the intercom.

'Get Inspector Toye along, will you?' he said.

Toye appeared within a few minutes. Pollard looked up as he came in.

'I've just had the call from Sydney. The chaps there have covered a lot of ground. We've now got the facts about Ash's return visit to Sydney after the Brinkleigh solicitor handed over his legacy from Clara Firth. He seems to have been pretty full of himself and looking forward to putting his feet up in England as a chap of independent means. Apparently it's quite definite that Rendell didn't leave Sydney until about a month later. He gave out that he was going over to Malaya about a job there he was interested in, but he obviously meant to come back. Paid the rent of his flat for three months in advance and left several hundred on deposit at the bank. Flew to Singapore but booked a flight to London for the following day. A rather inept attempt to cover his tracks from the look of it. It seems to me that our best move is for you to drive up to Brinkleigh and try to pick up his trail there. Remember the bank manager saying that a chap had come in and asked if they could give him Stephen Ash's address, a friend of his that he wanted to look up? Take the photographs of Rendell's body and see if anybody at the bank is able to identify them with the chap ... I note the gleam in your eye.

165

Just the day for a nice long run up north in the Rover, isn't it?'

Toye grinned and agreed.

'I'll get to the bank well before 5. Say half an hour there at most. Then some grub and a few hours' sleep and I'll be back here by 8.'

'With any luck that may establish Rendell's first move. Meanwhile I'll go along and see if they're getting anywhere in the science lab and probably have another go down in the Brading area. Good hunting!'

In the lab Pollard learnt that tests of some of the burnt substances brought up from the garden of Hob's Cottage were definitely a form of synthetic leather. A few strands of emerald green synthetic fibre had also survived the flames.

'Useful if the bloke you're after had a green shirt,' the scientist in charge of the investigation remarked. 'We'll let you know if and when we've anything more of interest to show you, Super.'

Pollard grinned, took the hint, and returned to his own department. While dealing with some urgent matters connected with another case his subconscious mind was occupied with the next step in tracing Rendell's movements after he had returned to England. Brinkleigh would have suggested itself as the most likely place for picking up Ash's trail. Toye would be getting there before long and contacting the bank manager ... Pollard took himself in hand, concentrated on the problem he was officially dealing with, finished it, and sat back to plan the rest of his day. He decided to drive down to Brading and contact Inspector Bosworth. It was important in connection with the case against Ash to trace the movements of Rendell as closely as possible from his landing at Heathrow until his death at Hob's Cottage. Somehow he had made contact with Ash.

Wouldn't a likely place for this be the racecourse at Westingham? The Sydney chap had been emphatic about Ash's enthusiasm for racing, and Rendell must have known this. They'd been buddies earlier on. Spurred on by this train of thought, Pollard embarked on the drive down to Brading and made good going. By a stroke of luck he ran into Inspector Bosworth on the steps of the police station and carried him off to lunch.

'What I'm trying to do,' he explained, 'is to track down what Rendell did after arrival at Heathrow. It seems pretty clear that he headed for Brinkleigh and somehow got on to the fact that Ash had made for this part of the world. I suggest that Rendell came on down here and soon discovered that there's an important racecourse out at Westingham. The Australian bloke I've been in touch with emphasised Ash's enthusiasm for racing very strongly, and after all Ash and Rendell seem to have been at least on friendly terms originally and may have both been keen on racing. So I think I'll go out to Westingham myself and see if I can possibly pick up anything useful.'

Inspector Bosworth agreed that this seemed worthwhile, and undertook himself to see if he could find out with the help of his chaps when Rendell had turned up in the area and where he had lived.

'What I hope to be able to show,' Pollard said, 'is that Rendell came over to England with the express purpose of running Ash to earth and making him disgorge some of the cash he'd inherited. I've always felt that in his turn he had some sort of hold over Ash, but had been made to carry the can over a job in Sydney that they'd both been in together.'

After some further discussion and undertakings to keep in touch the two men parted company, Pollard heading for Westingham racecourse. He located it without difficulty about seven miles from Brading. A large notice-board announced the date of the next meeting. The main entrance gates were shut but cars parked inside indicated that work of some kind connected with the course was in progress. Pollard parked outside and went in through a wicket gate. Looking about him he saw that the stand and the general complex of buildings appeared to be in excellent shape. He stood admiring the wide sweep of rolling downland and the well-kept race track. Some small groups of workmen appeared to be carrying out some repainting and other minor jobs, and two men were approaching along the track, one in a suit and the other in open-necked shirt and flannel trousers.

'Having a look round?' the former asked as the pair come up to Pollard. 'We're rather proud of Westingham, aren't we, Steve?'

'That's right, sir,' the other replied. 'And if you'll excuse me I'll just go along and get that repair to the railings going.'

'Sure. See you later. Your first visit here?' he went on, addressing Pollard.

'Yes. I had some business in Brading and thought I'd make a brief detour on my way back to Town.'

'You don't strike me as a racing man, if I may say so.'

Pollard made a lightning decision.

'I'm not,' he said, extracting his official card and proffering it.

His companion's eyebrows rose.

'The Buckford case, I take it? Come along to my office and have a drink. I'm David Hurrell, the managing director of this set-up.'

The office was admirably appointed and had a comprehensive view over the course. Pollard briefly explained the purpose of his visit to the Brading area.

'At the moment,' he said, 'we're working on the possibility of the chap drowned in the well being Ash's former business partner, George Rendell. If he was, he probably arrived in this area on Ash's track shortly before his death. According to the Sydney police they were both keen on racing, and used to go to meetings at a place nearby before they ran into trouble and Rendell was jugged. There apparently wasn't enough evidence against Ash. Relations between the two have been strained ever since. Then, as you'll have read in the papers, Ash came into money from a great-aunt which may have put ideas into Rendell's head. I came along here on the chance that someone might remember having seen him around ... It's not a pretty sight,' Pollard went on, taking an envelope from his pocket, 'but these are some post-mortem photographs after the bloke had been in the well several days.'

David Hurrell examined them in silence.

'I've absolutely no recollection of having seen the poor devil,' he said, 'but it isn't very likely that I would have. There's just the chance that he came over solo as you have today, and got talking to one of the men working on a job. I think it's just worth showing these photos to Steve Norris, the chap who was with me when we met you. I'll get him along.'

After a telephone call and a short interval the man who had been with him earlier on presented himself.

'Come along in, Steve, and sit down,' David Hurrell said. 'This gentleman's not a casual stroller. He's Detective Chief Superintendent Pollard of Scotland Yard who's in charge of the Ash enquiry, as you've probably seen in the local rag, and he thinks we might be able to help.'

Stephen Norris's face registered fleeting incredulity followed by intense interest and gratification.

169

'My, sir, it's great to meet up with you,' he exclaimed. 'My wife's a crime fan and follows every case of yours as gets into the papers.'

'Fine,' David Hurrell said, 'so you'll be genned up on the Ash case. You take on, Chief Inspector.'

Pollard briefly outlined the Yard's interest in George Rendell, a former partner of Stephen Ash, and the past connection between the two men.

'We've reason to believe that Rendell came to the UK recently in order to contact Ash and settle an old score,' he said, 'and we have picked up his trail which could have led him here. Both men are known to have been keen race-goers. These photographs of the body we found in the well aren't particularly pleasant but I'd like you to have a look at them.'

Steve Norris studied the photographs carefully.

'Sorry, sir,' he said, 'but I've absolutely no memory of seeing this chap around. We get pretty good crowds up here.'

'Do people ever wander in to have a look?'

'They're not supposed to, but it's difficult to keep all the gates locked when work's going on. Lorries come to deliver loads and so on. You came in yourself by a wicket gate, I reckon, sir?'

'Quite true. I was looking round and spotted one open.'

'It might be worth asking the chaps on jobs near the entrance if they've recently noticed any stranger about,' David Hurrell suggested.

The three men went down and approached half a dozen workmen touching up the paint on the grandstand. Brushes were dropped with alacrity, and after Pollard had been introduced and regarded with keen interest the purpose of his visit was explained and the photographs circulated. A man of about 30 reacted immediately.

170

'This bloke was 'ere right enough,' he said. 'Say early last week.'

'What makes you remember him so clearly?' Pollard asked.

'Twas this way, sir. I'd gone over to the store for a fresh can o' paint and found 'im lookin' around. I asked 'im what 'e wanted and 'e said 'e was a visitor from overseas — mind you could 'ear that, the way 'e spoke, bit like a Yank — and was there a programme o' races comin' off soon? This is 'im, I'd swear. Fawn colour trousers 'e was wearin', and a green shirt, bright like. Any good, sir?'

'It could be a lot of good,' Pollard replied. 'Watch the local paper. Thanks.'

In the meantime Toye was having a highly enjoyable day northward bound. A first class driver, he enjoyed getting the uttermost out of the Rover while keeping strictly within the limits of the law. He allowed himself half an hour's break for a snack at a pleasant-looking pub and arrived in Brinkleigh shortly after 4 o'clock. At the Northern Counties Bank he presented his official card and within a few minutes was shown into the general manager's office.

'I'm deputising for Superintendent Pollard, Mr Swan,' he explained when they had exchanged greetings. 'It's the Ash case once again. You'll have read about the body of a man having been found in a disused well in Mr Ash's garden, I expect?'

'I certainly have, Inspector. The staff are following developments with tremendous interest. What can I do for you this time?'

'Rather an unpleasant job, I'm afraid, sir. Superintendent Pollard wants you to look at these photographs of drowned men and see if you recognise the man who called here not long before our last visit and asked to be given Mr Ash's address.'

171

As he spoke Toye spread out half a dozen photographs on the manager's desk. Mr Swan scrutinised them carefully, selected one and passed it to Toye.

'This is the chap who called here,' he said. 'I'd swear to it in court if necessary. I went out to the front and had a conversation with him and offered to send on a letter if he'd care to write one to the bank to which we'd transferred the money Mr Ash had deposited with us while he went back to Australia to settle up his affairs.

'Did you say that it was a bank in Brading?' Toye asked. The manager hesitated momentarily. 'No, but I'm afraid one of my staff did when he handed in the letter over the counter. Without thinking and meaning to be pleasant to a customer she made some remark about sending it off to Mr Ash's bank in Brading right away. One of our senior staff heard her and reported it to me. I cautioned her, of course, but I didn't feel it was necessary to take any further steps. The chap didn't press the matter. Just wrote a few lines and handed them in for forwarding as I'd suggested.'

'I can quite see that it wouldn't have struck you as a matter of police interest,' Toye said. 'Anyway you mentioned to the Super when we called in again that you'd had an enquiry from a man who said he was a friend of Ash's and wanted to contact him when we called here for the second time, didn't you? You've nothing to reproach yourself with, Mr Swan.'

By arrangement Pollard and Toye met at the Yard early the next morning to discuss any progress made on the previous day.

'All that girl at the bank did was to speed things up,' Pollard said. 'Personally I'm grateful to her. I wonder what Rendell would have done if she hadn't mentioned Brading and he'd no idea where Ash had decided to settle? Well, I had quite a useful day, too.'

He went on to describe his visit to the Westingham racecourse and the information from the painter about the recent appearance of a chatty bloke in a bright green shirt who had said he was from overseas and wanted a programme of forthcoming races. 'It's not conclusive, of course,' Pollard went on, 'but just another pointer to where Rendell could have managed to run Ash to earth. I wonder —' He broke off at a knock on the door leading ot his secretary's office and shouted to the latter to come in.

'A message from the science lab, sir,' the latter reported. 'They may be on to something that might interest you if you'd care to go along.'

As they hurried in to the lab a few minutes later they were aware of an atmosphere of jubilation. Dr Fothergill the general director of scientific investigation carried on at the Yard was engaged in animated conversation with Roger Poland, one of the senior scientists, and a prosperous-looking man whom Pollard recognised as the managing director of Freemantle & Winter, the well-known firm of opticians. Introductions were made, and Dr Fothergill indicated the bench at which he was standing. On a white cloth was a pair of spectacles, the glasses of which were cracked but the pieces had been re-assembled with meticulous care.

'This little lot was near the bottom of the muck you dumped on us, Pollard,' Dr Fothergill said. 'We got Mr Everett of Freemantle & Winter to come along, and he's re-assembled the cracked lenses and has been able to reconstruct the prescription for the pair. By luck the chap they were made for had an abnormality in the right eye. So we phoned the prescription to Sydney and hope the chaps there can track down the optician who made the glasses up. Useful for identification purposes, what?'

Three days, seemingly interminable, elapsed while enquiries were carried out in Sydney. Pollard was at his desk trying to clear up arrears of work on other cases when the expected call came through at last.

'Wal, we've got what you want, Mr Pollard,' came the now familiar and slightly nasal voice of the police officer who had been in charge of the Ash-Rendell enquiries throughout. 'Firm of opticians who prescribed Rendell's spectacles and made 'em up two years back. Care to take the gen down right now? We'll confirm by air mail right away.'

The AC, on hearing the gist of the telephone call, leant back in his chair and contemplated Pollard sardonically.

'As I've remarked before, you're a lucky devil, Pollard,' he remarked. 'Those two boys having a half-holiday and seeing Ash belting down from the top of the ridge after the scream and crash of poor unfortunate Emily Gover going over the edge. Now a couple of Brading chaps spotting recent digging in Ash's garden. Not that you haven't the flair to know which leads are worth following up. What do you propose to do next?'

'I suggest we make the second charge against Ash specific, sir. Replace "wilful murder of person unknown" by "wilful murder of George Rendell and the concealment of his body in a well in the garden of Hob's Cottage". Presumably he'll have to appear before the Brading magistrates again for a formal charge?'

The AC agreed.

'Go ahead then, Pollard, and keep in touch.'

Returning to his office Pollard summoned Toye and briefed him.

'Put through a call to the Governor's office at Brading jail,' he concluded, 'and say we'll be down by mid-afternoon. I'll just cope with a few loose ends here and join you at the car in half an hour.'

174

They drove down to Brading in a relaxed frame of mind.

'End of Stage One,' Pollard remarked. 'The only snag is I can see myself having to spend the hell of a lot of time in court when the autumn assizes get going.'

On arrival at Brading prison they were informed that the Governor would like a word with Chief Superintendent Pollard before he interviewed Mr Ash. On arriving with Toye at the Governor's office Pollard was aware in a flash of an impending disclosure of major importance. As greetings were exchanged and comfortable chairs indicated his mind ran over the case of Stephen Ash at lightning speed.

'Smoke?' enquired the Governor, proffering a silver case. 'No, you don't, I remember. Well, Mr Pollard, a rather unexpected development. Stephen Ash has announced his intention of pleading guilty to the murder of Emily Gover. He asked for an interview with me this morning. I needn't tell you that there's no grape-vine to equal the inmates of a prison, and there have been hints and guesses in the press, as you know. A couple of young boys seem to have been got at. At all events Ash admits to the Gover murder. He's extraordinarily cool and collected about it. He killed her, he says, to prevent her from disrupting his carefully laid plan of blackmailing John Morley and other members of the family and feathering his nest to a degree he'd never dreamed of.'

Pollard sat, briefly speechless.

'Good God,' he exclaimed at last. 'What about the second charge — his murder of Rendell? We've the evidence now to make this charge specific.'

'My guess is,' the Governor replied, 'that he'll plead guilty on this one, too. I assume he hasn't the remotest chance of acquittal on either charge.'

'I rather think,' Pollard said, 'that this is the first time

175

in a long and ill-spent life that he hasn't been able to get away with it, and prefers to condemn himself rather than be condemned by a jury. There was his desertion of Fenella, for instance, and the opening it gave him in the long term to cash in on her lack of honesty. And that business in Sydney which ended in Rendell going to jail while he himself got off. Just two examples that happen to have come our way.'

Stephen Ash was committed for trial at the autumn assizes. On neither of the charges did the defence offer any evidence, and he was sentenced to 25 years' imprisonment in each case, to run concurrently, in view of his age.

The Morley clan endured the almost intolerable publicity stoically, heartened by the support of their many friends. Its massive scale drowned the occasional discordant snide remarks and poison pens. And clouds began to lift as the year ended. David John Morley, son of Richard and Gail, was born on Christmas Day, and Charles Adrian Morley in March. The families gathered at Glade for Easter. One evening as they sat around the library fire after dinner, the door ajar to catch a possible wail, Rose announced that she had had a great idea.

'How about the August Bank holiday for this year's Easter party?' she suggested.

If you have enjoyed this book and would like to receive details of other Walker Mystery-Suspense novels, please write for your free subscription to:

Crime After Crime Newsletter
Walker and Company
720 Fifth Avenue
New York NY 10010